# A FALLOW GRAVE

*Haunting Avery Winters Book 3*

## DIONNE LISTER

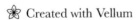

# CHAPTER 1

Ms Pearce was eighty if she was a day. And boy was she "creative." The fact that she'd sketched Finnegan's and Bailey's faces onto full-frontal bodies when I was pretty sure they'd never posed nude for any artists, well, I couldn't come up with any other summation, at least none that were polite.

I pressed my lips together, hard. If I laughed, she'd only be insulted. In fact, she had great skill—the likenesses were uncanny, the details... um... also very lifelike. I cocked my head to the side. Were the likenesses generous in certain areas? Hmm, I'd probably never know, but I was never going to look at those guys the same way again. How was I not going to laugh every time I saw them?

I lost the fight with my lips and grinned. Wait till they saw the pictures. Would they be creeped out or think it was funny? Should I even tell them? I raised my phone and took photos of the framed pictures on the white studio wall. I could decide later, but I was totally showing Meg. There was no way I could keep this to myself. I briefly wondered who the other poor sods were and whether any of them had actually posed for her. "And can anyone buy these?" I was pretty sure the boys would have something to say about that if they were for sale.

Her eyes widened, and she put a demure hand on her chest, as if she hadn't been the one to draw those pictures. "Oh, no. Of course not. These are part of my private collection. I do commissions, of course, and I also sell landscapes, but only my closest friends and I enjoy these." She smiled, a creepy twinkle in her eyes. "I never married, you know. I prefer to have flings. These new apps have made life very interesting. You'd be surprised who swipes right on me." She winked.

"Ahhhh, okay." I did not want to be surprised. This was more than enough unsettling information for one day. Had Finnegan and Bailey swiped right? Is that why their likenesses were there? *No, stop. Don't go in that direction; you'll hurt your brain.*

"There was this one man. That one there." She pointed to one of the paintings. "Ah, the things he could do with his—"

"Um, look at that lovely duck picture! Did you sketch them and then paint them plein-air, or did you take a photo and work on them later? The *ducks*." I thought I'd better add that, just in case she decided I was talking about something else.

Ms Pearce giggled but thankfully turned and pointed a liver-spotted finger at the opposite wall, which was covered in colourful depictions of the local countryside in all kinds of weather. "I do sketch in the field, but I also take photos. I like to take my time and get the details just right."

"Well, they're beautiful." I wasn't joking. I snapped more pictures. "Can you stand in front of that wall, and I'll get you with the paintings?" I crossed my fingers, hoping she wasn't about to steer the subject back to the other wall again.

She adjusted her pink beret and whipped a lipstick out of her dress pocket, slathered the bright fuchsia on her lips, and smiled. "I'm ready when you are." Thank. God. The sooner I could do this, the sooner I could get out of here… and tell Meg what happened. My gaze strayed to naked Finnegan. *Stop looking, Avery. Bad girl.* Well, it wasn't really him, but how was I supposed to get that out of my head now? Should I tell the guys? Even if I did, they couldn't do anything about it, and as far as I knew, Ms Pearce wasn't breaking any laws. The real question was, could I look at Finnegan and Bailey without laughing?

I held my phone up towards the cheeky old lady. "Say cheese!"

Ms Pearce lived within a ten-minute stroll of the office, and since it was sunny, I walked. On the way back, I passed the tree where I'd first met Patrick, the young man who'd crashed his car and died. I gave a nod to the tree and smiled sadly, but there was no one there. Me convincing his friend Craig that the accident wasn't his fault and that Patrick didn't want him to forever punish himself had helped him cross over to where he was supposed to be. Hopefully he was enjoying his new "life."

As I continued into the quaint village of Manesbury, I could only marvel at how quickly my life had changed from despair to happiness. For the seven hundred and twenty-nine thousandth time, I basked in gratefulness. Coming here was the best decision I'd ever made… and gone through with. I didn't see myself as a particularly brave person, but that was one thing I could acknowledge I'd done that was worthy of the title. I would remember that for the future—being brave led to good things.

Two salt-of-the-earth-looking men on the wrong side of middle age stood facing each other on the path in front of me. I was going to have to ask them to move aside so I didn't have to walk on the road. I hated doing that, especially as it seemed they were in the middle of an argument.

It appeared as if the shorter of the two had had enough. He swore and said, "This is all I have to say to you, Graham." His middle finger flicked up, and he waved it around, the gold watch on his wrist glinting in the sun, then turned and stomped down the street with a hasty stride. At least I wouldn't have to ask them to step aside—there was room for me to pass now.

Graham called out, "You can't run from me, you old fool! We're not done yet." As I hurried past, he swore… obviously not at me. Well, I didn't think it was at me. His brown eyes, set in a weathered, deeply wrinkled face, widened slightly before he frowned, turned the other way, and walked off. His limp wasn't overly pronounced, but it was noticeable. Had the other man kicked him before I showed up, or was that an old injury? I guess I'd never know, which irritated me no end. Being curious—or was that nosy—was great for being a journalist but terrible in everyday life. You didn't always get an answer to your questions, and I'd wasted many hours before slumber pondering stupid things, the knowing of which wouldn't change my life in the slightest, except might lead to me getting more sleep.

I'd had a coffee at home this morning, so I bypassed the cafe. Now that I had to run a car, saving was even more important. Who knew when something would need fixing, and petrol wasn't exactly cheap. I also wanted an emergency contingent in case Mrs Crabby became too much and I had to find somewhere else to live. She'd kept to herself the last few days, but that could be because she was saving her energy for an almighty blow-up. One never could tell.

At work, I let myself in. Bethany and I ignored each other; then I made my way upstairs to my desk. Just another Tuesday morning. The eventful walk here had me forgetting all about those paintings… until I saw Finnegan at his desk. He looked up at me as I came in. "Morning, Lightning."

My cheeks heated with the image from this morning. He had clothes on, but I still had to bite my bottom lip against the laugh that tried to escape. "M-morning, Vinegar."

He narrowed his eyes. "What's so funny?"

I turned my back on him to place my things on my desk. Since seeing that naked pic, I couldn't unsee it. When I saw Finnegan, it was as if I knew I'd seen him naked, and, well, I wasn't mature enough to deal with that. I really needed to grow up. What was I, twelve? Turning, I cleared my throat and wrangled myself under control. "Ah, nothing. Just thinking about a funny meme my friend sent me just before I walked in." So he wouldn't ask me about the meme, I changed the subject. "How was your date last night?" Monday was a weird night for a date, but Finnegan had explained he did it on purpose with all new women, in case he didn't like them. Having work the next day was a good excuse to leave early, apparently. If anyone asked me out on a weeknight, I was going to say no. It was obviously a sign of a player.

He smiled. "It went well. We bypassed dessert and went back to her place. I got home late." He tapped his pen on the table. "Might even see her again."

I sucked in a mock shocked breath. "Do I hear wedding bells?"

He snorted. "Ha ha, very funny." He put his hand up in a stop motion. "And before you say anything else, yes, I know I hardly ever do second dates. I'm trying to grow as a person."

I grinned, but then that damned painting popped into my head. I blushed. Oh sheesh. "Ah, is that it?" I hastily sat and took my laptop out of my bag and opened it.

He gave me a weird look. "Yeah, that's it. You're acting weird today. You're not upset that I'm going on a second date, are you?"

My head jerked around, and I stared at him with panicked eyes. "Oh, God, of course not!" I might have been a tad too enthusiastic because his eyes registered rejection. Oops. "Not that there's anything wrong with you. You know I would never date a work colleague. That's all." *And I don't want you knowing I think you're hot because that's just asking for trouble.* I was patiently waiting for my crush to disappear. If only things like that didn't take so long.

He smirked, as if he knew better. Damn him. "Just checking."

Carina flounced in, her long blue hair out and bouncing against her back. "Morning, lovelies. How are ya?"

I smiled. "Great thanks. I love your dress." She wore a pinafore-style in deep purple. The dress ended just above her knees, and she'd finished the look off with bright-purple Doc Martens. If only I could pull off such a cool look. If I wore something like that, someone would be sure to ask if I'd just come from working at the circus.

She grinned as she sat. "T'anks. I made it. I make most of my clod'es."

"Oh, wow." It made total sense, since she loved to cover all the crafty things for the paper. "I'm impressed. I have trouble sewing buttons on. In fact, I have a shirt I haven't worn for a year because I couldn't be bothered sewing on the button that fell off."

She laughed. "Oh, you're such a dill. I'll sew it on for you."

I was not going to be that pathetic. "Ha, no way. I'll get around to it… one day. I'm sure if Vinegar can go on a second date, I can sew a button on a shirt." I smirked, knowing she'd give him hell.

Carina spun to face him. "Oh, Finny, you didn't!"

He gave me a "thanks for nothing" look and waved a dismissive hand. "Well, not yet, but I'm going to. Why's that such a big deal? She's nice, and I want to see her again."

Carina raised a brow. "And when was d'e last time you went on a second date? It was about six mont's ago, if I remember correctly."

"Give or take."

"So, maybe you're growing up?" She stood, leaned forward, and patted him on the head.

He brushed her hand away. "For Pete's sake. I'm not a dog." He gave me the evil eye. "That's the last time I tell you anything."

I stared at him, all innocence. "Will you at least invite us to the wedding?"

He ripped a piece of paper from his notebook, scrunched it in a ball, and let fly at me.

I smirked. "Ha, missed by a mile." His phone rang. "Saved by the bell."

Finnegan picked his phone up and looked at the screen while Carina giggled and sat back down. Finnegan gave us each one last dirty look before heading for the door and answering his phone on the way out. I sighed. "I guess that's my cue to get back to work." I'd decided not to show Carina the photos because, well, I figured it was bad enough that one of us wasn't ever going to be able to look at him with a straight face again. Plus, if she knew, she might tell him, and he might confront the artist. I still wasn't sure if she deserved being confronted. Maybe I'd talk about it with Meg later.

"Ha, me too. I have t'ree articles to write. It never ends." Her smile told me that she was happy to be busy, and to be honest, so was I.

After an hour, I had my article on Ms Pearce done and submitted, minus any mention of nudes. Shortly after I sent it, Mr MacPherson called my mobile. Gah, I hoped I didn't have to rewrite any of it. I hated thinking I was finished with something, only to have to keep working on it. "Hello, Julian." And I still wasn't used to calling my boss by his first name.

"Hello, Winters. Would you mind coming to my office? There's something we need to discuss." His tone was more serious than usual.

My pulse thudded in my neck. What had I done? "Ah, yes, of course. Be there in a moment." He hung up without saying goodbye, which was normal but seemed more sinister after his order for me to come see him. Carina was still working away as I left and didn't so much as move her gaze from her computer screen. Which suited me just fine because I didn't need to tell her I was about to get in trouble with the boss.

As I made my way to MacPherson's office, I replayed all my recent interactions with people in my head. Had one of my interview subjects complained? My forehead scrunched. There was no one who'd seemed upset with me, and I hadn't written anything mean about anyone. I hadn't even done a third message from the dead yet. Had Bethany complained about me ignoring her? Which was kind of stupid since she started it.

I stopped at MacPherson's closed door, took a deep breath, and knocked.

"Come in."

I pushed the door open, then closed it behind me. No need for anyone else to hear whatever dressing down I was about to get. If only dressing down was dressing gown. I'd much rather he handed me one of those because I was employee of the month and waved me on my way. Being delusional had its uses.

I sat. "So...." I didn't want to ask what I'd done wrong because what if, by some slim margin, I hadn't done anything wrong. Then I'd just look guilty, like I expected to be caught for something.

He clasped his hands and rested them on the desk, then, either thinking better of it or not being able to contain his energy, he freed them and grabbed a pen with one hand and tapped it against the other. "I'm not quite sure how to speak to you about this, so I'll just jump in."

I blinked. Not the most comforting of starts. *Please don't fire me.* Going home now would kill me. I'd been here long enough to know that I loved it here and it was the best thing I'd ever done for myself. Being jobless meant a one-way ticket home. I maybe could've stayed for a few weeks and holidayed, but I'd be returning home with less than what I arrived with and would end up back with my parents. Acidic nausea spiked up my throat, and I spied a bin next to MacPherson's desk. That's where I'd vomit if circumstances called for it.

MacPherson's forehead wrinkled. "You look a little green, Winters. Is everything all right? You're not going to be sick, are you?" He rolled his chair away from his desk until he hit the wall behind him.

"It depends on what you're going to say. Am I fired?"

"Why do you always think you're going to get fired?"

"You're not firing me?"

"No. Well, I wanted to chat to you first and clear something up, but I don't think I'm going to fire you."

That was supposed to reassure me? I cleared my throat and swallowed. "What did you want to clear up?" Erin, the young office ghost, appeared in the chair beside me. Her gaze pinged between MacPherson and me before settling on my face. She gave me a reassuring nod and patted my thigh. The coldness seeped through my skin, and I shivered. I gave her the most subtle nod ever—if I wasn't careful, I'd look like I was two sandwiches short of a picnic, nodding and smiling at a vacant chair.

He brought his hands together on the tabletop again, and his thumbs circled each other in a distracting dance. "I received a phone call this morning… from Australia."

I jerked my gaze up to his face as my stomach dropped. My mouth dried. Speech function disappeared, left behind by my racing brain.

My parents. It had to be. What had they told him? Why had they called? This couldn't be happening. *Please be wrong, Avery.* Maybe it was just my old boss seeing how I was going?

As far as dramatic pauses went, this one was going to kill me. My mouth finally caught up to my head. "So, who was it?"

"Your mother."

I bit my tongue. *You are not going to cry, Avery. You're an adult. Whatever she told him, you can set the record straight. Play it cool.* "Oh, okay." I took a slow breath. I wasn't going to let them ruin my new life. Calm and collected was how I was choosing to be. I ignored my racing heart and relaxed my face. What MacPherson didn't know…. If I appeared flustered, whatever my mother had said might be believable. She was likely trying to paint me as a crazy person, so I had to act as uncrazy as I could.

He stared at me, maybe waiting for me to crack. But I wouldn't. Never again.

My tone was as casual as a guy in a bar doling out a bad pickup line. "Oh, how… strange. How is she?"

He narrowed his eyes, maybe attempting to discover any cracks in my façade. "She told me about some… issues you had before you came here." Another pause. I wanted to slap him and tell him to just tell me. Why was he making me draw it out of him?

I sighed. "Can you just tell me, please? I have work I need to get back to." Maybe a bit of honesty and candidness would work in my favour? "My parents are… difficult people. They didn't want me to move here. Me making my own decisions doesn't sit well with them. If my mother rang to criticise me and undermine me to my boss, well, it wouldn't surprise me. She might have framed it as being worried about me, but that won't be it. Whatever she told you, does it make sense given how I've behaved and conducted myself while I've worked here?"

His thumbs stilled, and he folded his arms. "No. You seem rather rational to me." His brow wrinkled. "Is it true that you spent time in a mental-health facility?"

How was it that a stomach could drop even after you thought it had hit rock bottom? He wouldn't be able to confirm that information due to patient privacy laws, and how dare my mother tell him. It wasn't her place. Blazing anger torched the crop of nausea that had taken space in my belly. "No." I'd taken the hospital paperwork when I'd left. I'd thought about burning it, but I kept it as a reminder to never trust them. Ever. Since my parents had no proof, I was pretty sure my lie would go undetected. "My parents like to sabotage my life. This is one example, and I'd rather not talk about any others."

"So it's not true that you're schizophrenic? You don't hear voices or see things that aren't there? You don't have sudden urges to hit people?" Only sometimes. Now, apparently.

It took everything I had not to scream. Frustration curled my hands into fists, but I forced myself to relax. "No, it's not. Even if that were true, if it isn't affecting my work, firing me would be discriminatory. And I also don't want to indiscriminately hit people." If I were to ever hit anyone, it would be because they more than earned it. My expression had gone from relaxed to firm. He had to know that I wouldn't take this easily. I did have to be careful not to get too testy though. He just wanted to know the truth. It wasn't his fault my mother was a psychopath. Why was it that people always believed the evil person over the good?

"So, you're not on medication?"

"No, and I don't see or hear things that aren't there... not that it's any of your business." Yay that I was sticking up for myself. The only problem was, he might see it as me being rude. Maybe he'd fire me after all. Erin patted my leg again, and I held in a shudder. "Look, I'm sorry for being upset, but you can see my position, no? My mother, who I don't get along with, calls my new boss and says horrible things about me and tries to get me fired. This is not only embarrassing, but it's also unethical. If my work performance is not up to scratch, or if my behaviour with my colleagues is unacceptable, then you have cause for concern. I don't appreciate being called in here to be grilled over hearsay and what would otherwise be privileged information." People with mental illnesses deserved more respect. I'd bet there were plenty of people who were managing their illnesses with no one any the wiser, and that's how it should be. And where was my support if I did have health challenges? I was good at my job and treated my work-mates with respect. That's all that should matter. I could feel an article coming on.

He cleared his throat. "Your work performance is exemplary, and I've had no complaints from anyone. I just wanted to clear this up. I'm sorry if I've overstepped the mark. Are we good?" His earnest expression held regret.

I blinked. He could probably see a lawsuit coming, or maybe he was actually a decent person? Whatever, I wasn't going to make any waves, but I also wasn't going to let my parents ruin my life. Not. Any. More. I shoved my fear of ending up back in Sydney with them aside. "Yes, we're good. As long as you don't accept my mother's calls. She's a toxic person who I don't want in my life. Ask yourself: What kind of a mother calls the other side of the world to get her daughter fired?" A niggle of pride smoothed out the rage. I'd stuck up for myself and made sense. Something I never thought I'd be able to do when it came to my parents.

His cheeks reddened, and he nodded. "Yes, of course. Also, I'd appreciate it if you didn't tell Kelly or Walsh about this. As you said, this should all be private." Hmm… if I didn't know better, I'd say he didn't want to look bad, but to be honest, this situation made us both look bad in different ways. I didn't want everyone questioning my sanity, which was what they'd do if this got out.

"Of course, Julian. Consider it forgotten already."

"Good-oh."

I gave him a fake smile and stood. "Well, if that's all, I'll be going."

He smiled. "Have a good day." Wow, right. Sure thing. After that meeting, today was going to be sketchy at best.

Out in the hallway, I contained the urge to slam the door after myself and shut it quietly. Erin looked up at me. "Are you okay? Your mum sounds awful."

I gave her a sad smile and whispered, "I'm fine, and yes, my mother is next level. Thanks for caring."

She grinned. "Any time. If you need me, just call out." She waved and disappeared. What a sweet kid. Her kindness made me feel a bit better, but I couldn't help dwelling on how horrible my parents were. Why couldn't they just leave me be? And what were they going to do next? I wasn't going to call and let them know they'd gotten to me because they'd take glee in it. In fact….

I hurried back to the office. Carina had left, and Finnegan wasn't back either. Perfect—I wouldn't have to try hard not to vent or have to explain what MacPherson wanted. I grabbed my phone and pulled up my mum's number. Block. Then I brought up my dad's number. Double block. I sucked in a huge breath and sighed it out again. Done.

Did I think ignoring them would work? No, unfortunately. It might even make them more determined to stuff my life up. But if I'd learned anything over the last year, it was that you had to make the most of every day, and today could be the last day I had on this earth. Today, tomorrow, and however many days I had left, I was going to make the most of them. And no one was going to stop me.

# CHAPTER 2

After covering two other boring stories while lugging my anger at my parents around, by five, I was tired. There was no way I was cooking dinner. I'd earned a treat, so a dinner out at Meg's pub was on the agenda. I went home and showered so I could just fall into bed later. By the time I walked into Meg's, it was just after six. Loud chatter greeted me. For a Tuesday night, it was pretty busy. Bailey waved at me from behind the bar, his toothy grin enough to make me smile. And then I remembered that painting, and heat ambushed my cheeks. *Get a hold of yourself, woman.* I visualised Ian kissing the tree. Yep, better than a bucket of cold water.

I headed over. "Hey, Balls... I mean, Bails. How's it going?" *Argh, seriously, Avery?*

He gave me a quizzical look. "Good. How are you?"

I pretended I hadn't just had a poo-filled day or called him Balls. "Good thanks. I'm in the mood for a glass of house white tonight."

He winked. "Coming right up." I managed to hold my sigh in until he'd turned to grab a glass and the bottle from one of their many fridges. Bailey and Finnegan weren't the only attractive blokes in this village, either, and many of the women were pretty too. There must be something in the water. Whilst I wasn't looking to start anything—the call from my mother today was a good reminder of the disaster that was me and Brad—eye candy was a nice treat, and I'd never say no to that. A quick visual of the painting popped into my brain. Argh! *Ian kissing the tree.*

Someone elbowed me in the arm. I spun around, ready to take them on. Meg held her hands ups and laughed. "Hey, don't punch me, Miss Hapkido." I'd told her about my love of the sport and how my old instructor had sent me a few instructional videos. I was practicing every second day and then filming the results to send back and get feedback on. It didn't cost too much, and it meant I wouldn't lose touch with where I was at. When I needed to practice rolling and falls, I did that on the grass in Mrs Crabby's backyard since my apartment wasn't laid with soft mats.

"Hey, how's it going?"

"Great, thanks." She smirked and lowered her voice. "I noticed you checking out my brother's backside." If only she knew the half of it. Maybe I shouldn't tell her about those paintings. Hmm, not today. She might feel obliged to tell her brother.

Before I could try and deny it (busted), Bailey put the wine glass on the counter. "Here you go." Hopefully he didn't hear what Meg just said.

I ignored the blush heating my cheeks and gave him some money. "Thanks."

He put his hands on his hips and stared at the money. "I can't accept that."

"Yes, you can. If you don't, I'll stop coming in and asking for stuff. Please just take it." I hated being a charity case. I could look after myself, and even though they meant it in a nice way, I didn't want to rip them off.

His hazel gaze stuck to mine, and it was as if the noise and other patrons disappeared—cheesy, I know. Was he going to say something? This eye locking was way too long to not be flirting. My heart rate kicked up in a good way (for a change). He blew out a breath and shook his head. "One of these days, you're going to let me give you something for free. Seriously."

Meg was staring at us with a pleased look on her face. All she needed for this to be a real show was for her to be holding popcorn. I kept waiting for her to say something, make a joke about Avery and Bailey sitting in a tree.

"Maybe one day. I just don't like to take advantage. You and Meg have been so kind, but I'm an adult, and I can pay for my food and drink, especially when you guys have a pub to run." I ignored the fact that he was probably asking me out or seeing my reaction to the potential asking out. Part of me would've loved to have him take me on a date, but the other part would've hated it because it could all go wrong, and I had to see him all the time.

Plus, I wasn't ready.

There was no point jumping into another relationship when I didn't even know where I was at by myself. I still needed to get to know myself, which was happening, but it took longer than five minutes. And my family was a mess. Dragging someone else into that twilight zone wasn't fair. He rolled his eyes and took the money. I smiled. "Thanks. You're the best." Okay, so I had to give him something. Way to be confusing, Avery. Before anything else could come of it, I took my glass and turned to Meg. "Table for one?"

She looked at me like "what am I going to do with you?" "Right this way." I followed her to the far wall where she put me at a two-person table. I sat, and she did the same, pinning me with eyes that radiated that she wasn't going to take any nonsense. "Okay, I wouldn't normally get involved, but Bailey really likes you, and I can tell you like him. Why not go out on a date?"

My mouth dropped open, and I ignored the butterflies in my stomach and the desire to ask how she knew he liked me. Reality won out—why did she have to go there? I sighed. Might as well be honest and hope she understood. "I like Bailey, too, but, Meg, I'm not ready to date anyone. I just got out of the relationship from hell, and I need to know who I am. Besides, what if we did date for a while but then had a massive fight and broke up? Where would that leave us? Not to mention, I'd be running into him all over the place. I can't deal with that drama right now. I'm still recovering from my old life."

"You'd make a great sister-in-law." She grinned.

"Yeah, I know. So would you. But can you just… drop it? Maybe let him know I'm not ready for anything with anyone. If I miss my chance, well bad luck to me."

She turned and saw what I saw—a gorgeous brunette with glossy hair to her waist and shapely calves—chatting him up. She leaned against the bar, placed her elbows on it, and squished her boobs between them to better display her cleavage. Bailey, like the normal hetero guy he was, appreciated the show. At least he didn't glue his eyes to them. He looked for an acceptable amount of time, then took her order. Meg turned back to me. "She's moving in on your man, Avery."

I laughed. "He's not my man, Meg. And maybe she'd be better for him. I have enough baggage to sink a cargo ship. Trust me: it's better this way." Regret wiped the smile from my face. We definitely had chemistry, and I knew he wasn't Brad —he was far from it. But I also knew right now, it was a bad idea. I gave Meg an earnest look. "I'm sorry. I really am. Bailey's awesome." *But I'm not.* "If it happens one day, it happens, but please don't push it."

She frowned. "You're a party pooper. You know that?"

I smiled. "Yes. It's my goal in life to poop as many parties as possible." We laughed because that sounded as silly as it was. How did one even poop a party?

She blew a raspberry at me. "Right, well, now you've ruined my week, I have to get back to work. What are you having?" She stood.

"I'll have the fish and chips, thanks." It was one of the cheaper things on the menu, but I also happened to know they had a great supplier of fresh fish, and it was always delish.

"I'll order it for you. You can pay on your way out."

I raised a brow, about to argue if she was trying to give it to me free.

She held her hand up. "Don't worry. I'll make sure you pay. Ha ha. I'll come back later and say hello when it slows down a bit."

"Okay. See you then." I raised my glass of wine at her, then took a sip. Mmm, fruity.

Dinner soon arrived and I enjoyed every bite as I people watched. All kinds of people frequented the pub. Well-dressed older couples, people my age kicking back after work in business clothes, and older labourers threw back a beer or tucked into a meal or enjoyed a cocktail. The people at the table next to me sounded like German tourists if their conversation was anything to go by. I'd done some German in high school, so I could at least pick the language, but I couldn't understand a word of it. Thanks, Frau Morris, for doing a substandard job.

Raised voices that sounded aggressive had me turning my head. Two men had just pushed out chairs and stood chest to chest at a table. A guy, late twenties, his dreadlocks somewhat contained in a red-and-black-striped knitted bandana shook his head. "You can't! Why? I'm your best worker. You said so last week. Please, mate, don't do this."

The ambient chatter dissipated, like someone turning off a tap. Everyone was here for the spectacle.

The older guy was someone I recognised—the farmer-looking man from this morning. He had hands on hips, and he looked at the ground before staring at the younger man. "I'm sorry." He licked his lips. "It can't be helped. I'll give you a good reference."

The young man shut his eyes, and his shoulders slumped. Then he opened his eyes, poked the older guy in the chest, and swore, telling the old guy where he could shove his reference. He snarled and raised his fist, then thought better of it and lowered his arm. "I'm done. You've screwed me. You know that, don't you?"

Bailey appeared out of nowhere and put a hand on the young man's shoulder. "Alfie, bud, it's not worth it. Come on. You're better than this." That name was familiar, but I couldn't remember why. I hadn't met him before. My brain was fried after being hit by lightning, but my short-term memory wasn't that bad… at least I didn't think it was.

Alfie turned brown eyes Bailey's way. Defeat shone from them. "Yeah, man. I'll go." Without another look at his adversary, he left, his feet shuffling dejectedly towards the rear exit. Bailey made sure the old guy was okay, and then he pulled out his phone, put it to his ear, and made his way back behind the bar.

So, what was the old guy's story? That was two altercations in one day, and I'd happened to be there for both of them. Had he had others as well? Had his day been worse than mine?

Rather than sit back down, the old guy pushed his chair in and left the same way Alfie had. I glanced at Bailey, who was serving someone. Maybe someone should go out the back and make sure nothing escalated, in case Alfie was still out there.

Meg walked over. "Hey, what just happened? One of the servers came into the kitchen and said there was a fight."

"It wasn't a fight so much as an argument. Bailey shut it down. Both men have left, but I was just thinking since they both went out the back way that maybe someone should check on the car park, make sure they're not going at it again. One of them was young, and one was old. The old guy might not come out of it well." I stood. "I can go. You're busy."

"Maybe just stand at the back door and look out. Let me know if anything's happening. If they're still arguing, might be worth calling the police."

"Okay. I'll be right back." I picked up my dirty plates from the table. "I'll drop these into the kitchen on my way." I grinned.

"Want a job here?"

"If you need help, hit me up. I waitressed when I was a teenager." My parents were stingy, and if I wanted new clothes or anything that wasn't essential, like food, I had to pay for it myself. At least it meant I was good at budgeting.

"I'll keep that in mind. Now go, just in case someone's getting beaten up."

I didn't think that was actually happening, but you never

knew. I walked quickly, put the plates in the sink to the surprised stares of the kitchen staff, then jogged to the back door.

A hazy summer evening lit the car park. It was illuminated enough to see without street lights. Bitumen, cars. That was it. No men. No fighting. Phew. My curiosity being what it was, I went back inside, told Meg nothing was happening, then went to the bar. "Hey, Bails. Who were those men?" Maybe there was some kind of scoop with the farmer guy? At least he looked like a farmer. Had his crop been bad this year? I had no idea about farming, growing food, producing milk or wool. He'd obviously fired an employee. Or maybe he was doing well, and the guy was a terrible employee, but he felt bad about letting him go because he was such a nice old guy?

"The young guy was Alfie—we grew up with him. He's had a rough trot but was coming good." Bingo. He was Finnegan's friend who'd stayed at his place when he was getting his life back together. "The old guy was Angus Donigal. Owns a farm about ten minutes from here. He gave Alfie a job when no one else would."

"That's sad that he just fired him then. Do you think Alfie will be okay?"

He wiped the bar with a cloth and bit his bottom lip. "I don't know. He's been clean, but something like this could tip him back into old ways." He stopped wiping and met my gaze. "I called Finn, let him know. He's closer to Alfie than me. He'll go see him soon, make sure he's okay."

"That's good. You guys are awesome, taking care of Alfie."

He shrugged. "I'd hope someone would do the same for me if I was down on my luck."

The stunner from earlier sidled up next to me and smiled at Bailey. "Hi, Bailey. Can I get another mojito?" She actually batted her eyelashes and did that jerk-of-the-head thing to flip her hair off one shoulder. Oh, God, spare me.

"I'll see you later." I gave him a sly smile and went to find Meg. After saying goodnight to her, I made my way home. Although I didn't know Alfie personally, I couldn't help but feel sorry for him. I knew what a struggle life could be, and I feared my own rug-pulling moment. Coming here was the start of me taking control of my life, but things could go south pretty quickly if one thing went wrong... like if my parents managed to convince my boss I was crazy. Then I'd lose my job and my working visa. And I didn't know if I could handle going back to Australia. Desperate circumstances called for desperate measures. I just hoped Finnegan's friend would be all right, because I could relate to how he must be feeling.

We all needed a bit of a break sometimes. The problem was, we didn't always get it.

# CHAPTER 3

"**A**very! Avery, wake up! Hurry!"

"Hmmm." I pulled myself from a dream in which I was eating Milo with a spoon directly from the one-kilo tub. The crunchy, teeth-clogging, malty chocolatiness disappeared. The part of me that realised I wasn't going to get fat because they were dream calories was happy; the other half panicked because someone had urged me to wake up. "Huh?" I blinked in the dark.

"Avery, something bad's happened." It twigged in my half-asleep brain that it was Charles's voice disrupting the darkness.

"What happened? Also, I can't see you. Can you do something about that, or do I need to turn the light on?"

"Sorry." Charles glowed, like I'd always imagined ghosts could. At least one of my assumptions turned out to be true. Because his glow was otherworldly, it didn't illuminate anything in my room except him. "Mr Donigal's been hurt."

I sat up, willing my brain to grasp onto the words. Donigal... "Oh, the farmer? The one with the horses you like to visit?"

"Yes. I went to visit the horses, and he was lying on the ground, like he was asleep, except there was blood on his face. I couldn't tell if he was breathing."

I slid out of bed and turned on the light. This was a situation I needed to be fully awake for, and sitting in the dark wasn't conducive to waking up. I checked my phone. Just after two in the morning. I yawned and sat back on the bed.

"Well, are you going to do something? He needs help." Charles leaned from foot to foot, his body tense, as if he was ready to run.

"I don't know what to do. I could drive over there or call emergency services, but people would wonder how I knew. I can't tell them my ghost friend told me."

"Couldn't you pretend to be psychic or something?" His pleading gaze slapped me with all the guilt, and doing nothing about this also went against all my instincts.

"No, but there must be a way we can help him without getting in trouble. Maybe I can block my number from showing up, and I can call emergency services, get an ambulance there?"

"How am I supposed to know?"

"Oh, right." He existed in a time way before mobile phones, and I guess as a ghost, he'd never had to learn about them. "Was anyone else there? Did you see how he got hurt?" My memory was coming back online, and I recalled he'd had the argument with Finnegan's friend this evening. Had Alfie hurt him? Poo sandwiches. This didn't look good.

Charles lifted his hands and let them fall back to noiselessly slap the sides of his thighs. "Well, Avery? Are you going to help? I don't have anyone else to go to."

"There's only one problem—I don't know the address."

"It's off Longbottom Lane."

I chuckled, even though mirth in this situation was highly inappropriate. "Longbottom Lane? Who names your streets?"

"How the heck should I know?" He pressed his lips together and gave me a cranky look. "The longer we take, the more likely he'll be to die."

"Right. Sorry." I went into my phone settings and changed it to a silent number, then called 999 and, using the best English accent and lowest tone I could, I asked for an ambulance to Donigal's Farm off Longbottom Lane at Manesbury.

"What number?"

"I'm sorry. I don't know."

"Are you there now?"

"No. Please hurry. He's badly injured." Then I hung up and dropped my head. "She probably thinks it's a crank call." I lifted my head and looked at Charles. "I'm sorry, but that's all I can do. Do you want to go to the farm and wait for them? Let me know if they don't come soon."

"I can try, but I don't know what soon is. Remember?"

"Does anyone else live there? Maybe they'll realise he hasn't come inside, and they'll look for him?"

"He lives there with his wife. His adult son's there's sometimes too. Maybe they'll realise. I hope so. In the meantime, I'll go and wait for the ambulance. As soon as they get there, I'll come back and let you know what happened."

"That would be great. Sorry I couldn't do more." I gave him my most regretful facial expression. Then he disappeared.

Right. There was no use trying to go back to sleep until I heard from Charles, so I went to the kitchen and boiled the kettle. Some chamomile tea would be nice.

"Can I have some too?" Everly sat up and looked at me over the back of the couch.

"I thought you didn't need to lie down or sleep."

"I don't, but sometimes I like to pretend."

"Fair enough." What would it be like, not to ever get tired? Right now, that sounded fantastic. I yawned again. "So, do you want me to pour you a cup and set it on the table so you can pretend you're going to drink it or were you just joking?"

She sighed. "I was just joking. I miss it though... tasting things, feeling the texture in my mouth. Death isn't as bad as I thought it would be, but it's not as good as it could've been either."

"I'm sorry. I wish I could change things for you."

"Meh, don't worry. So, why are you up?"

I explained the bit about Charles waking me up and why. I didn't go into anything else though. I was tired and not in the mood for long conversations. Besides, Finn's friend probably had nothing to do with it. Hmm, did I really believe that? Where's there's smoke there's fire isn't a clichéd saying for nothing. I'd also love to know what the argument he had with the other guy in the morning was about.

Charles appeared, standing next to the kitchen table, his eyes wide. "He's gone."

I stared at Charles. "What?"

"When I went back, Mr Donigal was gone. I looked around for him but couldn't see him anywhere."

I sighed. Woken up for nothing. "He probably came to and went inside to bed." I stared longingly at my bedroom door-way. "To sleep." How I wished I was asleep. "Oh, week-old squashed banana."

Everly chuckled. "What?"

"I called an ambulance for him. They're going to turn up, and he won't need help."

Charles cocked his head to one side. "Maybe he still needs help. Just because he took himself to bed doesn't mean he doesn't need medical help. He looked pretty beaten up, and he's an old man."

"Can you go back and report on what happens?" Now that I was invested in what was going on, I wanted to know the ending.

"Okay, but I won't be able to go inside."

"I don't care. Just wait there till the ambulance comes and they go inside. Then wait for them to come out again. Maybe they'll put him in the ambulance and maybe they won't. At least we'll know he's okay. If they bring him out in a body bag, well, then…."

"Well, his ghost wasn't there, so he's probably alive." Charles's voice held a hopeful note.

I nodded. "Probably."

"Okay, I'll be back." He vanished.

The electric kettle had boiled and clicked off, so I poured the water into the cup and let it steep while I sat on the couch next to Everly. We chatted about her day while we waited. And here I was, initially worried I'd be lonely when I moved here by myself. How wrong I'd been. It was actually rare that I felt lonely because I knew one of my ghostly friends was only a call out away. I sometimes found myself wanting more alone time, though—they tended to be there when I didn't call and least expected it… like tonight, or was that this morning?

Charles still hadn't returned by the time I finished my tea, and I didn't feel like another one, so I decided to go back to bed. Charles could wake me up again… if I even managed to fall asleep, but it was worth trying. I said goodnight to Everly and slipped back between my sheets. Before I shut my eyes, I checked my phone. 3:37 a.m. If Charles returned soon, and I managed to fall asleep by four, I'd get another three and a half hours. That would be good.

But things didn't work out that way... of course.

I had just drifted off, or what felt like it, when Charles was back. "Avery, are you awake?"

Argh. I opened my eyes to a glowing spirit. "Kind of. What time is it?"

"How should I know?" Thanks for nothing.

I fumbled on my bedside table and found my phone. Four sixteen. I'd managed maybe twenty minutes. I guessed it was better than nothing. "What happened?"

"The ambulance people came and knocked on the house door. Mrs Donigal answered. She said she hadn't seen him, that he'd been out drinking and hadn't returned home. She stuck her head out the door to look at something, then said his car wasn't even back. She wasn't even worried and told them he sometimes went on all-night benders with mates."

A dull ache formed around my eyebrows. "I could get into trouble if they manage to trace my phone." I was pretty sure they couldn't, but you never knew what technology had been invented until it was too late. I would've asked Charles if he was sure about what he'd seen, but I knew he wouldn't do something like that as a joke. Which meant that something was not as it was supposed to be. "Do you know what his car looks like?"

"Nope. I don't take notice of stuff like that." He looked at the ceiling for a moment and folded his arms, likely thinking. He finally looked back at me. "I do remember seeing one of those large cars with a tray back, and there's a rusty-looking square car, grey. I don't know if either of them were there. What do you think happened?"

"I have absolutely no idea. Maybe he went back out again?" As I said it, I knew it didn't sound right. Had someone knocked him out and moved him somewhere else? Charles hadn't seen his ghost, but had he died? Had he been murdered and dumped? And how was I supposed to alert the authorities? As it was, if he turned up dead or was reported missing, my phone call would be scrutinised. If Sergeant Bellamy listened to that call, he might recognise my voice. Thank goodness I decided to put on an accent and change my tone. Who knew if it was enough to throw him off. All I knew was, if things went south for Donigal, it better be, or I was going to be in a world of trouble.

"Why don't you go back to the farm and have another look around, maybe hang around the house, see if you can hear anyone talking. If he doesn't turn up, you'd think his wife would call the authorities. If that happens, we need you there to listen to the conversation." Even though Bellamy had warmed to me since the last murder investigation had proven that I was helpful and he was willing to work with me, things wouldn't happen quickly, and he was still going to give information to Finnegan. I had to be on the ball if I wanted an article out of this—if there was one to have. The more important thing was, though, if this ended up being a case that needed solving, I might be able to help.

"Okay. I'll check back in with you later today, if something happens."

"Great."

He hesitated before leaving. He looked at me with sad eyes. "Do you think he's okay?"

I shook my head. "I'm sorry, but I don't know. Maybe he'll

turn up in the morning and everything will be fine." I gave him an encouraging smile that I didn't feel. But we had to be positive. I hated catastrophising, and this could just be a case of a night out gone temporarily wrong.

After Charles left, and I shut my eyes again, I ignored the fact that Mr Donigal had two confrontations in the hours leading up to Charles seeing him on the ground. If I put two and two together, I was going to get four, and I didn't want that when there was nothing I could do without admitting I could see ghosts or was psychic—basically admitting I was nuts. After the stunt my mother pulled with MacPherson, that was the last thing I needed.

As I tried to drift off to sleep, I apologised to Mr Donigal for not being able to do more. We couldn't always step up and be the people we should be, and I had an inkling that if something bad had happened to the farmer, I would carry the regret around with me for a long time. Unfortunately, there was nothing I could do about it.

!

# CHAPTER 4

I didn't have any interviews booked until eleven, so I dragged myself out of bed at nine. I'd taken ages to fall asleep because a few thoughts kept repeating and feeding the guilt. I wasn't sure what time I'd fallen asleep— whatever time it was, it hadn't been early enough. I picked the sleep from my eyes and stopped dead, narrowly avoided smashing into the doorjamb. Oops.

While I was making coffee, Charles appeared. He didn't bother with any niceties. "The police turned up this morning. Mrs Donigal called them. When they turned up, she told them at the door that he hadn't returned from being out last night. She said the last time she'd seen him was just after five thirty, when he left to meet Alfie for dinner. I checked around near the house, and that square car wasn't there, but the big one with the tray at the back was. I looked, and it said Isuzu. It's a blue car with big tyres and four doors."

"What did the police say?"

"They're going to look for his car. Mrs Donigal gave them a description. She said it was a grey 2009 Land Rover Defender with a hardtop."

I sat at the kitchen table and opened my laptop, then looked up the model. "Hmm, it is rather squarish, or maybe rectangular. It's a blocky kind of car. Here, look at this." It was very similar to Meg's car.

Charles peered over my shoulder, and I shivered at the subtle draft and coldness. When ghosts were right next to you or touching you, it was as if a door between worlds had been left ajar, and the air of the dead filtered through. My instincts screamed at me to run, but my brain knew Charles, and it overrode my amygdala. *Sorry, amygdala, maybe next time something happens, I'll let you have your way.* "Should we go look for it?"

"I'd say yes, but the police are probably out there searching for it, and since he was at the pub, I can't see him driving too far away. They're likely to have found it if it's anywhere we'd look. Manesbury isn't that big. Plus, I don't have time to drive around aimlessly, hoping to find a car on the side of the road. It could be anywhere." Poor Charles. I wasn't being helpful at all. "Is there any way you can float above the land and fly around?" If I was a ghost, I'd at least want to be able to fly. There weren't many benefits to dying—well, practically none —but you'd hope that was one of them.

"I can fly, but it wouldn't work. When we do that, every-thing down below gets blurry—the higher up we are, the worse it is. It's hard to monitor how fast you're moving, and it makes us go really fast. I could stay close to the ground, and it would be okay, but it would still take me ages because I can't get an aerial view." He hung his head for a moment, then looked at me. "Maybe I'll go to the police station, see if

Sergeant Fox will help. Could you come with me? He likes you."

Poor Charles was still scared of the man, and I didn't blame him. It was only last week that we'd all come to an understanding and cleared up that Charles had really had nothing to do with Sergeant Fox's murder. The fact that I saved his great-grandson from killing himself also endeared him to us. "You'll be fine. If you have any dramas, find me. I think I'm going to visit the farm under the guise of doing an article on the missing local man. Maybe putting something online today might help find him, like an appeal for information, or if anyone's seen him." Hmm, that was a good idea. Hopefully, I hadn't missed my chance and MacPherson hadn't heard about it and assigned something like that to Finnegan.

He gave me a worried look, then disappeared. I grabbed my phone and called MacPherson. "Hi, it's Avery."

"Morning, Winters. Are you calling in sick?"

"Ah, no. I'm calling because I wanted to see if I could get clearance to do a video interview with Mrs Donigal for an appeal for information on her missing husband." I crossed my fingers, hoping I still had the scoop.

"What? How do you know Donigal's missing?"

Oh, yeah, right. "I can't give away my source. I promised not to say anything. Anyway, can I?"

There was a looong pause. "I'll have to confirm he's missing first. Come into the office. I'll talk to you when you get here."

Why did it always feel like I was in trouble? "Ah, okay. I'll be there in fifteen."

He hung up, as usual, without a goodbye. I wanted that interview, so I raced to get ready, and because I was putting this on video, I made sure my hair and make-up were on the better side of decent. When I was done, I was the epitome of a sweet young woman you'd want to tell all your problems to. Hopefully, Mrs Donigal would give me some extra information about her husband's relationship with the men he'd argued with yesterday.

As I hurried down my stairs, I had the unfortunate luck to pick the moment that Mrs Crabby was coming out of her door. She had a wheelie trolly thing for her groceries and the most dishonest handbag I'd ever seen over her shoulder. It was bright yellow and said, "I bring the sunshine wherever I go." Maybe it was the kind of sunshine that caused melanomas and scorched the earth till it turned to desert?

She looked up at me and frowned. "You're leaving late today. Are you unemployed already? Because if you are, you'll have to leave. I'm not a charity."

Wow, so many assumptions. She had as much faith in me as my parents. I bit back all the rude retorts that popped into my head—I needed this place. Gah, being beholden to people was frustrating. "I still have my job. In fact, I'm going to interview someone right now about their improved gut health. They've started eating other people's poo. Apparently it makes them feel wonderful. I'm curious as to how they handle the consistency and if they mix it with other food, like, say, they could make a cheese crap. Like a crepe only crap, get it?" She stared at me, her mouth closed. Her hand came to her mouth, and she gagged. I gave her a serene smile. "I was also w—"

Her eyes flew wide, and she shook her head. "Don't say another word. This topic is disgusting. You Australians are so uncouth." I sent a quick apology to all the good people of my nation that I was misrepresenting. Mrs Crabby opened the door and left on tentative legs. Every reminder that she had arthritis and was in pain made me feel guilty, but then again, she always had to start something. Why was that? I shrugged. Oh well. Maybe she'd learn, eventually.

I locked the door behind me and easily caught up to Mrs Crabby. As much as she irritated me, since I was driving Daisy to work in the hopes I'd get that interview, it would be horrible of me not to offer her a lift. I could live with that regret rather than the guilt of not having asked her. "Would you like a lift into the village? I'm driving today."

She narrowed her eyes at me—probably wondering if it was a trick question—then threw her disdainful gaze at Daisy. "In that thing? Are you sure it won't break down?"

I shrugged. "I have no idea, but I hope not. Besides, it's downhill to the village, so we can roll. I *think* the brakes are good, but you never know. Are you feeling lucky today?" I gave her a genuine smile because this situation couldn't be any stupider. She needed a lift, and I was offering. Hopefully, under all her bluster, she knew a good deal when she saw it.

She gazed down the laneway, probably calculating how long it would take her and how much it would hurt against having to trust me and my car. She looked to the heavens, as if to say, "why must you punish me so?" before returning her irritated face to me. "All right, but if anything happens, you can pay for a cleaner and any specialists I'll need."

I wasn't agreeing to anything. Should I even be taking her? What if she decided to fake an injury getting out of my car or something? Hmm, I was probably in more danger giving her a lift than she was.

Despite my misgivings and pre-regret, I opened the door for her and stood by in case she needed help. After folding her trolley thing, I put it in the boot and got into the driver's seat. Being a good neighbour, I hoped the powers that be repaid me with that interview I wanted. "Where would you like to be dropped?" I asked as we drove down the laneway.

"The post office, please." Her request was polite enough, so I'd forgive her for gripping the door handle for dear life. Thankfully, the trip was uneventful. I helped her out of the car and gave her the trolley before parking down a laneway near work. That had gone better than expected—she hadn't berated my driving, which was the most positive thing I could say about her thus far since I'd come to England.

I applied lip gloss and checked that my hair was behaving before getting out of the car. Yep. All good. *Let's do this, Avery.*

Striding into the office like I owned it was a good start. Before that confident mindset disappeared, I went straight to MacPherson's office. The door was open. I knocked, and he looked up from his computer screen. "Winters." He smiled. Phew. After yesterday, I wasn't sure what kind of reception I'd get. Who knew if my parents were going to keep trying to get me fired? I always had to wonder what they'd told him. Did he doubt my word, and was he quietly wondering when I was going to lose the plot? It was a shame that ghosts couldn't read minds. That would've made my life, and solving crimes, so much easier. "Come in." He gave a nod at the chair.

Erin appeared on one chair, smiled, and waved. "I'm here for you, Avery." She was so sweet. My own cheer squad for meetings with the boss. After yesterday, she must've thought I needed backup. I smiled at her, then directed it at MacPherson because, well, for obvious reasons.

"So, does the story check out? Has Mr Donigal been reported missing?"

He pushed his chair out from his desk and stood. "Yes, it

does check out." He walked around his table and sat again. Okay. And I was worried about being the weird one. Arms folded, he leaned back in his chair and peered at me. "How did you know?"

"I told you—I have a source who seems to know what's going on around the village. You know that's privileged information. I can't tell you."

He pouted. "You haven't bugged the phone at the police station, have you?"

Who did he think I was? 007? "No. I'm not a trained spy." Although, if my parents managed to ruin this job for me, maybe I'd approach the English government and see if I could train for MI5 or 6. Either would be fine. I'd get a new identity, and my parents would never find me again... unless I wanted to be found. Hmm....

He narrowed his eyes and stared at me, as if weighing up the likelihood of whether I was a spy or not. "Right!" His arms flew forward, and he slammed his hands on the desk. I started. "I've called in Smyth from our Exeter office. He's one of our best on-location cameramen. He'll meet you at the Donigal farm in around twenty minutes with all the equipment you'll need. Have you done video news before?"

"A couple of times." I wanted to say I wasn't a professional —so he wouldn't get his hopes up—but if I did that, he'd probably tell me not to do it. "On camera, do you want me to introduce myself as being from the *Manesbury Daily* or your main news station?"

"You can say *Manesbury Daily* and MacPherson Media. That way, we can share it across all our mediums."

"Any other advice?" I was here to learn, and I'd rather he told me anything obvious I might miss instead of disappointing him later.

"Here's the address of the farm and Smyth's mobile number." He handed me a piece of paper. "Oh, and see if you can get her to cry on camera. Hysterics are always good." He smiled, and Erin laughed. That kid had a weird sense of humour. "Right, off you go. Good luck."

Ah… I was still stuck on making the missing man's wife cry, but okay. I stood. "Thanks, M— Julian. I appreciate this opportunity." Before he could take it back, I hurried out of the room, Erin, skipping along behind me. Rather than stopping to see if Carina or Finn were in, I kept going. I didn't want Finn hijacking my story. Hopefully he was busy working on whatever other dramas were happening today that Bellamy had to deal with. As I was going down the stairs, I whispered a goodbye to Erin.

She waved enthusiastically. "Bye, Avery. Have fun making that lady cry!" She faded away, her laughter echoing for a couple of seconds. Well, that was creepy. I shuddered as I walked past the reception area and out the front door.

The drive to the farm took about seven minutes, give or take. It was situated at the top of a quintessential rolling hill. An open gate fronted the road, the entry to a long gravel driveway. I stopped there, turned off the car, and waited for Smyth. Should I have called Mrs Donigal before coming? What if she wasn't home? Maybe we could just look around, get some footage, but would that be considered trespassing? We could always do a segment right here. Not great, but better than nothing. Would Smyth be angry he'd been called all this way for nothing? Probably. There was nothing I could do about it now. MacPherson hadn't said to call her, which maybe he should have. But then again, he was paying me for my time, so it didn't hurt to try. If we asked for permission, she might have turned us down and we'd miss out on an exclusive. News was bound to get out sooner rather than later, and we wouldn't be the only news station here.

A beat-up blue Ford sedan pulled up on my right. I got out to the smell of cow manure. *Lovely.* The driver's door of the Ford opened, and a fifty-something-year-old man got out and looked at me over the roof of the car. His side-parted, shortish salt-and-pepper hair stuck up at weird angles. Had he just gotten out of bed? He looked me up and down. When he greeted me, he did so without a smile. "I'm Smyth. You must be Winters." Talk about no-nonsense.

"Yes. Pleased to meet you." Just because he wasn't particularly polite, didn't mean I wasn't going to be. I'd do me, and he could do him. Plus, I didn't want to get on his wrong side because I needed his help, and who knew when I'd have to work with him again?

"What are we doing?"

He was obviously a seasoned cameraman—I doubted you got into this job at his age, and he seemed very comfortable—but he was deferring to me, the new girl on the block. That was different. Usually any men I worked with wanted to take the lead and tell me what to do. Whether they thought they knew better than me or it was habit, who could tell? In this case, I wasn't going to give him room to doubt me. Even though I wasn't sure if it would work out, I stood up straighter and made sure my tone was full of "I've got this" vibes. "We'll drive up, and I'll knock on the door and explain why we're here. She doesn't know we're coming, but I have it on good authority that she's home."

He gave me a sceptical look, and whilst he didn't question anything, he grunted. Not exactly an encouraging response.

I gave him a nod. "Let's go." There was no point worrying

about what he thought. This would turn out how it turned out. I got in the car and took a deep breath. *Let's do this, Avery.*

The house sat about a hundred and fifty metres from the gate—I still estimated most distances in metres, but I was doing my best to use feet as much as I could. It took a while to break the habit of a lifetime. My tyres crunched as I parked in the large gravel area at the front of the single-storey stone house. A dark blue four-door car with a tray at the back and a red Mazda sedan sat outside, which was a good sign. One must be the other car Charles had told me about. The other might belong to a friend or relative who'd come to support Mrs Donigal.

Opposite the home, about forty metres away, was a concrete-block, metal-roofed building with a wide, high-clear-ance opening that looked to contain stables. That must be where Charles hung out with the horses. Beyond that shed was a double-height timber barn. A red tractor was visible through the double doorway. To my right was a gate leading to a field. A couple of horses grazed with a herd of cows. Yep, it was a farm all right.

I slid out of the car and ran my hands down my grey pencil skirt. I'd paired it with a sky-blue sleeveless top and grey jacket. My outfit was a bit more formal than what I usually wore, and I'd applied heavier make-up than usual, although it was still fairly neutral. The thought of being on video was terrifying, but hopefully the camera wouldn't be on me much, if at all. We were here to get Mrs Donigal's reactions to the situation.

Smyth got out of the car. "Give me a couple of minutes to set up. If she's home and willing to talk, I need to be ready to go straight away."

"Okay." Might as well check out the stables. Even though

we were potentially trespassing, I wanted to see where Charles spent some of his time. I'd be fibbing if I said I wasn't keeping my eye out for a clue. If he'd been lying on the ground last night, there might be some evidence. I slid my phone out of my inside jacket pocket.

I wandered to the barn, my court shoes noisily grinding the small stones together. At the entrance to the stables, I let my vision adjust to the darker interior. Had the police searched the farm, or did they assume he wasn't there because his car wasn't?

Inside was a large, open area with hay bales and bags of feed stacked on the floor. Tack hung from one wall. A broom and rake were splayed on the floor next to the wall, which seemed odd, since everything else was in order. Maybe a gust of wind pushed them over, or maybe something happened in here last night, and they were knocked over in a struggle. Okay, so I was jumping to conclusions. I was just trying to think like a detective... not that I knew how they thought.

I took a few photos and then took a closer look at the floor to see if there were any blood stains. There were bits of hay, but that was about it. I took a close-up anyway because you never knew. I turned my attention to the five stalls lined up along the back wall. Three were occupied. I smiled and approached a huge bay with the longest eyelashes. "Hello, gorgeous. Can I pat you?" I tentatively lifted a hand near her nose so she could smell me. Once she'd done that, I rubbed her nose. She nudged into my hand. Either she liked it or she was hoping for food. "Sorry, gorgeous, but I don't have anything for you."

"Avery, I'm ready."

I turned. Smyth stood at the door, camera on his shoulder.

I went to him, and he handed me a microphone. "You can use this. I'll tell you when I'm rolling."

"Okay, thanks." I felt more professional holding the microphone. A smile formed on my face. Journalism took many forms, but this felt more real and important than the usual work that I did—not that it was. How weird that I had that perception. I guessed we were all sold on the fact that if you were on TV, you were better than everyone else. How silly I was. The work I did was important—whether I was writing about the story or filming it, there was no difference. *You are not inferior to your television cousins.*

He followed me to the house but stood back while I knocked on the door. A dog barked from inside. If it was an attack dog and Mrs Donigal wasn't the friendly type, I was in trouble. I knocked again and stood back, ready to run. Should I take my shoes off? Court shoes weren't the best for making a quick getaway. Hmm, I could also hit the dog with them if I was desperate. That was two votes for taking my shoes off.

The handle rattled, the door opened, and the barking stopped. An older man stood there, maybe early sixties, his grey hair combed neatly from his side part. His thin moustache had a wide gap in the middle—it was as if he had another set of eyebrows. "Can I help you?" His mouth brows were rather expressive when he spoke. I swallowed my mirth—it was highly inappropriate under the circumstances... as usual.

"Hi, I'm Avery Winters from MacPherson Media, more specifically, the *Manesbury Daily*. I wondered if Mrs Donigal was home. We know her husband's missing, and we wanted to help. Maybe she'd like to talk to us and make an appeal to the public?"

"I'll have to check with Pat. Just wait here a moment,

please." Mr Eyebrows for a Moustache shut the door. In my face. Right. This wasn't promising. I turned to Smyth and shrugged. He was smiling. Okay, so he enjoyed watching people get doors shut in their faces. Nice. I blew out a large breath and turned back to the door. Maybe MacPherson had let me come here without calling first because he wanted to teach me a lesson? Hmm, that didn't seem like him. Maybe he figured either I'd get a good interview, or I'd gain experience in what could go wrong.

"Bollocks!" I pivoted around at Smyth's outburst. His face was screwed up, and he was fishing around in his pants pocket. It was my turn to smile at the white semi-liquid running from his shoulder down the front of his T-shirt. Apparently, the birds were on my side. He pulled out a tissue and wiped his shoulder. When he noticed me smiling, he scowled.

The door opened. I dropped the smile and turned back around. A tall woman, who also looked to be in her sixties, stood there. Her wrinkled, tanned skin spoke of working outdoors. Her straight grey hair was pulled back in a loose bun. She didn't look like she'd been crying, but her face had a stony, closed look about it. Maybe she was trying to be brave and not give in to all the thoughts you'd have when faced with a missing husband.

I gave her a gentle smile. "Hello, Mrs Donigal. I'm Av—"

"Yes, yes, Bruce told me. You want me to ask the public for help. Is that it?" I resisted the impulse to step back at her no-nonsense manner.

"Ah, yes, that's it. We're hoping the public can help find your husband. It would be a big help to the police too. It won't take long. Maybe five or ten minutes. If you have the time. I imagine you're very worried and feel helpless. This is some-thing you can do that could make a big difference." Bellamy was going to love it if she complained to him about me bringing the police into it, but whatever. I was here for a story and to help, and, as usual, little white lies might help me get what I wanted.

"Well, I do want to do what I can. Yes. Please come in."

"Thank you." I turned to Smyth who was finished cleaning up, but there was a tell-tale smear where the bird poo had been. He he. I gave him a nod.

It didn't take long for us to set up in her living room. The blue carpet was worn in places, and the paint looked like it used to be white, but years of wear and tear had yellowed it in patches—it didn't appear to be from cigarette smoke because there wasn't that putrid smell. A pretty antique sideboard drowned under a tsunami of paperwork—a glance picked out a power bill, bank statement, and a flyer for carpet cleaning. "Where should I sit?" she asked.

I peered around and through a wide doorway. "Maybe at the kitchen table with your rustic kitchen in the background." Filtered light was coming in through her sheer yellowing curtains from the window opposite, which meant the light would be better than the living room, which was darker, and the kitchen table was tidy; the only things atop it were salt and pepper shakers. I turned to Smyth. "What do you think?"

"Looks fine."

Mrs Donigal went first, her left hip dropping with every step. Her male friend—or maybe brother or some other rela-tive—followed her rolling gait, his hand hovering near her lower back, ready to help if needed.

The dated kitchen was neat and tidy. There was a wood-burning stove and a farmhouse sink. So cosy. A round timber table with four chairs sat near one wall, and Mrs Donigal sat in one of the chairs, her support person sitting next to her. He looked at me. "Is it okay if I sit with her while she does the interview?"

"Of course." I moved one of the chairs away from the table and faced her. Smyth was standing to our right and could film either of us or both at the same time. Most of the time, the camera would be on our subject. I just needed to introduce us. I looked at Mrs Donigal. "At any time, if you're too upset, let me know, and we'll stop filming." She nodded. "Are you ready?"

"Yes. Okay." She had her hands in her lap, fingers linked, one thumb caressing the other. Her friend rubbed her back for a moment before lowering his hand. The dog padded in, his claws clicking on the tile floor, and sat at her feet. Aw, what a good boy. Animals were the best.

I turned to the camera, lifted the microphone, and took a deep breath. *You can do this.*

Smyth held the camera steady on his shoulder. "Rolling."

I did the intro MacPherson had asked for, briefly described the situation, then threw it to Mrs Donigal. "Can you tell us the last time you saw your husband?"

"Late yesterday afternoon… maybe five thirty. He was off to the pub for dinner with a mate. He does that sometimes."

"And when did you realise he was missing?"

"This morning, early. We get up at five—there's so much to do on the farm. And he wasn't in the spare bedroom. He sleeps there when he comes home late, so he doesn't wake me up." She looked at her lap and bit her bottom lip. Was she trying not to cry? Whilst crying would be good for ratings, I hated that she was upset. Her husband was missing. Not knowing would be hell.

"How long have you been married?"

She looked up at me, eyes glistening. "Forty-one years."

"Does Mr Donigal ever stay away this long without telling you?"

She shook her head. "No. He has responsibilities. This farm is his life. He would at least call and tell me so I could do the chores he couldn't." How much could she do with a bad hip? What would happen to the farm if he was dead? Would she have to move? Would she lose everything? Surely the son could help. And where was he? Shouldn't he be here helping his mother?

"Does he have any enemies?"

She shut her eyes for a moment, then opened them. "No. Why would he? He's just a farmer." A flicker of anger alighted on her face, and then it was gone. Yikes. If I offended her too much, she might stop the interview, and then I'd be in trouble.

"Did the police say where he was last seen?"

She nodded and sniffled. "The Frog and Trumpet pub. Having dinner with a mate. He was last seen leaving there."

"Is there anything you'd like to say to everyone out there?"

She looked at the camera. "Please, if anyone has any information, please tell the police. We need Angus to come home." "We" must be her and her son. She leaned down and patted the Australian cattle dog. Okay, so "we" might be her and the dog.

I turned to the camera as it swung my way and made one last appeal before signing off.

"Cut." Smyth lowered the camera.

"Thank you, Mrs Donigal." I stood. "Is there anything you need that I can help with?" We were part of the same community, so I might as well ask.

"No, but thank you for asking. My son will be home later. He had to go out and get some things done." She pushed herself off the chair, and her friend jumped up to help her.

"Things don't stop, even when tragedies happen. Life goes on." She gestured for me to move into the living area. I could take a hint.

We quickly made it to the front door and out. As soon as I said goodbye, she shut the front door. Maybe she wanted to burst into tears and didn't want to do it in front of us. MacPherson would be so disappointed. I turned to Smyth and handed him my microphone. "So what happens now? Do you send the information to the station later?"

"Yes. I edit the story, but I'll send both versions to MacPherson, and he can give me feedback on what he wants changed, if anything. I sometimes liaise with the reporter, but seeing as how you're inexperienced, we won't. Watch the footage later, and you'll get the idea how we do things." He headed straight for his car. I scanned the sky, hoping for another bird visit. Out of luck. Bummer. Just before he got in his car, he waved me over.

"What's up?"

"They always say that, you know."

"Say what?"

"In all my years of doing this, hardly anyone has ever said their loved one has enemies. Either they don't know their loved ones, or they're lying. But which one is it this time?" Profound statement completed, he winked, then slid into his car and shut the door. Conversation over. And what was I supposed to do with that?

Shaking off my irritation—even if he was abrasive, I'd gotten the interview I wanted—I hopped into my little ray of sunshine and started her.

"He killed me."

I jerked around to the man in my passenger seat and screamed.

Mr Donigal looked at me out of his good eye. His face was smashed in on one side, but I could still see his disbelief. "He killed me."

"Who? Who killed you?"

His one good eye begging for help, he faded away, leaving me alone with my racing heart and a sense of dread.

*Here we go again.*

# CHAPTER 5

Rather than go back to the office, I went straight home. Once I was safely in my living room, I called out to Charles. He didn't come immediately, so I opened my laptop and started a file on the case. I had to write an article to go with my interview as well, which would just outline the situation, but knowing what I knew, I might give it an ominous slant—there was no use giving people false hope.

After fifteen minutes, I called out again, "Charles! I've got news. Hello, Charles?"

He popped into the kitchen, directly into a chair opposite me at the table... which was still pushed in. "What is it? You're interrupting."

"So *sorry*. By the way, does that hurt?"

His face scrunched up. "What?"

"Does that hurt?" I waved at his torso, chopped at chest level by the table. Would I ever get used to these apparitions who looked so real yet could float through doors and walls and tables?

He looked down, then rolled his eyes. "Of course not. Look, if you don't have anything to say, I have to get back."

"I found Mr Donigal. He's dead. I mean... I didn't find *him*, just his ghost."

His eyes widened. "Where?"

"At the farm. Outside. In my car." I shuddered, remembering the state of his face. Charles slumped, and now he was up to his neck in table. My brain was doing somersaults, trying to process the information. *It's fine, Avery. It's just a ghost.* I would've started crazy laughing, but Charles looked so sad. "I'm sorry."

He sighed. "He was a nice man, you know."

"Where were you when I called? What did I interrupt?" Maybe changing the subject might help.

"At the police station with Sergeant Fox."

I'd hoped that was the case, but knowing his reluctance, I wasn't sure he went. "That's great. What did you find out?"

"They found Mr Donigal's car on the side of a back street, and they've interviewed three men. They were also talking about a call to the ambulance service last night. They played the tape." Yikes, that had been me. It would obviously look really strange now that he was missing, but I hoped me blocking my number from showing was enough to avoid getting caught up in this in a bad way.

I swallowed my nerves. "My name didn't come up, did it?"

"No. I think you did a good job changing your voice."

I sighed out a relieved breath. "Do you know who they interviewed?"

"Yes. One man was a garbage truck operator—Vic Peoples. One was just a man called Fredrick Brandt, and the other was a man who worked for him, Alfred Thomas."

"Oh dear. That's Finnegan's friend Alfie. I saw them at the

pub last night. Donigal fired Alfie yesterday. This doesn't look good." I frowned. Finn wasn't going to be happy. But had his friend done it? If he had, he deserved to be in gaol. "Did you watch the interview?"

He nodded. "Yes."

"What did they ask Alfie?"

"They asked him when the last time he saw Mr Donigal was, and he said at the pub. They asked him if he killed him, and he said no, of course not. As soon as they figured out that he was the last person to see him alive in the car park, as far as they knew, and that he'd been fired that day, they ordered a search of his house."

So I wouldn't forget any of the information, I created a new doc on my laptop and typed in all the names and everything Charles had said. "Unfortunately, that makes sense. Did the other interview subjects have anything interesting to say?"

"I don't think so. The garbage truck guy was there because after they found the car, they figured out it was garbage night and wanted to find out how long the car had been there. The garbage guy said he saw it there at five thirty this morning. Fredrick Brandt was the local bank manager. They were talking about money. I switched off because it was boring and there was a cat meowing outside that I wanted to go see."

I pressed my lips together, but it was no use; the smile came anyway. He was such a kid. Although, if I had to listen to financial information or look at a cat, I knew which I'd pick. "Right. Was there anything else you can think of?"

He stood, the table cutting him off at the waist. "Nope. I have to get back. I don't want to miss anything. I'll let Sergeant Fox know that you saw poor Mr Donigal's ghost." He sighed.

"Well, make sure you let me know of anyone else they

mention as a suspect or even just want to interview. If I can chase those people up, I might have some luck."

"Will do. Bye, Avery. I'll be back later." I opened my mouth to say farewell, but he was already gone.

I spent the afternoon finishing the article while running the case through my head. How could I pass on any information to Sergeant Bellamy without a) looking like the perpetrator or b) looking crazy? While I pondered that, my phone rang. "Hey, Meg, what's up?"

"Sergeant Bellamy was just here. He interviewed me and Bailey. Mr Donigal's missing, and we were the last people to see him alive… sort of. Maybe." I knew she was saying he might be dead and that the murderer would've been the last person to see him, but she didn't want to actually say it.

I would've acted surprised, but she might see the interview I did earlier. "Yeah, I heard. I spoke to Mrs Donigal today. She's appealing for help." I could let Meg assume that she'd contacted us, rather than the other way around. "Did Bellamy say what he thought happened?"

"No. He's still missing, and I don't think they've arrested anyone yet, but it doesn't look good for Alfie." She sighed. "Bailey had to tell Bellamy that he saw them arguing before they both left. I wouldn't be surprised if he raced to grab Alfie straight away."

"Do you think he could've killed him?" Better to ask Meg than Finnegan. She'd likely be more objective.

"I've known him for a long time, and no, I don't think so. Other than the drug and drinking issues, he's a pacifist. I know he's stolen in the past, but I've never seen him be violent, and he's been drunk here countless times over the years."

"Okay, it's good to get your perspective. Thanks."

"There was another reason I called."

I considered the long pause a bad thing. "I don't really want to ask, so I won't. Have to go now."

She laughed. "I'll tell you anyway. We're hosting a charity speed-dating night here on Thursday, and you have to come."

If I'd been eating something, I would've choked. Meg was the last person I wanted to let down, but I was going to. "No, but thanks for asking." And why did she want me to do that when she was gunning for me and Bailey? Maybe, with a bit of luck, she'd given up on that idea.

"Oh, come on. Pleeeeeease come. I don't want to do it by myself. Besides, we're raising money for youth suicide prevention. It's fifteen pounds to come, and that includes a free glass of beer or wine."

"I'll give you the money as a donation. And you won't be by yourself. You'll be in a room full of other singles. Oh, I think my kitchen tap just turned on by itself. I gotta go. Bye!" I hung up and chuckled. Poor Meg. If it had been something important, I would've gone, but that… just no. If I donated the money in lieu of going, I wouldn't even have to feel guilty. Maybe I'd tell Carina and Finnegan about it. Getting more people to go would likely make Meg happy.

A text came through. *You're not getting out of it that easily.* A grinning emoji punctuated her statement. Grinning, I responded with a sticking-tongue-out emoji.

My phone rang. I rolled my eyes. Was she not going to give up? But then I looked at the screen properly and answered it. "Vinegar?"

"Don't sound so happy to hear from me."

I laughed. "Sorry. It's more that I'm surprised you're calling. Are you upset that I parked in *your* spot again?" It so wasn't his spot—it just happened to be the closest one to our houses.

"I wish. I'm calling because I just watched your interview with Mrs Donigal—it's up. Julian said you got a scoop this morning. Would you be able to tell me who your source was?"

"No, of course not. Sorry."

He sighed. "I wouldn't normally ask, but Alfie—my friend —has just been arrested for it."

"Oh no. I'm sorry. That's awful."

Was that Bellamy's voice in the background? "Yeah, it is. But he said he didn't do it, and I believe him."

"Are you at the police station now?"

"Yes."

"Look, I still can't tell you. I'm sorry, but I can't." *Because you would never believe me.* "Besides, surely they had enough evidence to arrest him. They wouldn't do it just on circumstantial stuff." He didn't answer. "Vinegar, are you still there?"

"Yeah."

"Well, what evidence do they have?"

"They wouldn't tell me, and they won't let me talk to him." Bellamy must've cut him out because Alfie was his friend. It was good to see the police sergeant had boundaries when it came to giving Finn information. "Look, I know you see me as competition, and I am, but not on this. I promise to waive my right to any stories about this case. If you won't tell me who your source is, can you at least see if you can get me some information on what's going on?" Wow, the shoe was finally on the other foot. I could rub his nose in it and say "welcome to the club," but I wasn't a jerk.

"Um…." I made out like I was thinking about it because I

didn't want him assuming I was a pushover. "Yeah, okay. But how is that going to help?"

"Maybe we can figure out who really did it. I just can't believe Alfie could kidnap someone or kill them. Not that there's a body. Look, I need to help him all I can. We need to at least prove it might not have been him. So, are you really in?"

It was hard to say no to him at the best of times—gorgeous men had that advantage—but the fact that he was trying to help a friend made it impossible to say no. "Yes, yes, I'm in." *Please don't be something I regret.* I'd have to be careful about the info I passed on because this could go nuclear in my face. If I said too much or the wrong thing, he'd dismiss me as lying or as knowing the potential killer, and neither of those had a good outcome. There was one positive thing about this though —if Alfie wasn't the killer, maybe with both of us working on it, we'd figure it out. Hmm, it might be nice to work on a case with a live person for a change. Things I never thought I'd say number two thousand four hundred and fifty-six.

"Thank you, Lightning. You won't regret it. I promise. And you're helping a great guy in the process. Alfie's had a tough go of it, and the last thing he deserves is to be sitting in gaol for no reason. Maybe we could catch up at the office tomorrow, go through what you know so far? Will you be there first thing?"

My first appointment wasn't till ten thirty, so I had no excuse. "Yeah, sure."

"Great. I'll bring the coffee. See you at nine. Bye."

"Bye." I never thought we'd be allies in crime solving, but there you go. My new motto would be "expect the unexpected." Then I'd be ready for anything all the time. Right?

# CHAPTER 6

I reached the office just before nine the next morning. Charles hadn't been to see me again, which meant he probably didn't have any new information. I did get a text from MacPherson saying the police called and thanked him for spreading the news and asking for any witnesses to come forward. Apparently, MacPherson was pleased with the job I did, too, so phew. With all the worry about Alfie, I'd forgotten about the actual job I'd done.

When I walked into the office, Finnegan and Carina were already there, sitting at their desks, takeaway cups at the ready. "Hey." I smiled.

"Mornin', Avery." Carina returned my smile.

"Hey, Lightning. Come sit here. I've saved you a seat." He grinned at his silly joke and nodded at my chair, that he'd rolled all the way from my desk. I chucked my stuff on my table and went to my chair, where I promptly plonked. Finn handed me a coffee cup. "Low-fat cappuccino. No sugar."

"Thanks." I took a careful sip, in case it was super hot. "Mmm, coffee."

Carina laughed. "I've decided to help too. So it will be the t'ree of us investigating d'is time."

For some reason, relief relaxed my shoulders. Carina would be a good buffer between just me and Finnegan. Too much time alone with him, and I might get stupid ideas. While Bailey was gorgeous, and I enjoyed his company, sense of humour, and his relaxed demeanour, Finnegan had a magnetic pull and had more of an edge to him. If I was honest, they were both hard to resist, and the less time I spent alone with either of them, the better. Carina would keep the mood light... safe. I grinned. "So, are we the Three Musketeers, or more like the Three Stooges?"

Carina laughed. "Oh, d'e T'ree Stooges, for sure."

Finn looked at me, then Carina. "For once, I'm going to agree with you."

She rolled her eyes. "For once? Oh, Finn, d'is isn't d'e first time, and it won't be d'e last." She looked at me. "So, what have you got for us?"

I hurried back to my desk and grabbed my notebook out of my bag. I'd only put on there what I thought I could get away with. The full, unfiltered version was on my laptop. But there were some things I couldn't just explain away because of my "source." Like knowing he was dead and that he'd been bashed. Also, that his body, at some point, had been at the farm before whoever it was had moved him. At least, that was the assumption I was going with. I didn't think he recovered from his beating to walk or drive away, then die. From what Charles had described, the ghost of Mr Donigal looked the same as when he'd seen him lying there.

As I sat, Finn said, "So, what have you got so far?"

"You guys might want to write this down, so you have your own list to ponder over later." They both took my advice and got out notebooks and pens. "Okay, firstly, I was at the pub last night when he was last seen. He was there for dinner with Alfie, and he fired him." I looked at Finn to see if he had any questions, but he stayed silent. "Alfie was upset, but he didn't threaten Donigal. It was getting heated, so Bailey came by and broke up the argument. Alfie left, and Donigal left a minute or so later. A couple of minutes after Donigal left, I thought I'd better check the car park and make sure they didn't fight out there. When I went, there was only silence and a few cars. I didn't see anything untoward." They both scribbled stuff down. "Have you watched the interview I did with Mrs Donigal?"

They both nodded, and Carina said, "She looked genuine. How upset was she when you were d'ere?"

"Upset but not inconsolable. About what I'd expect. She's probably hoping he's still alive."

Finn narrowed his eyes at me. "You don't think he is?"

"I don't know. As I'm sure you already know, the longer someone is missing, the more likely they are to have died or been killed. My gut tells me he's dead, but I have no proof." I wished I didn't have to lie. It would be so much easier if I could admit to everyone that I could see ghosts and that the man was dead. It would save so much time, but... my life didn't work that way. Things had to be complicated, convoluted, dishonest. My secret was making me more of a liar than I already was. "Also, I saw Donigal arguing with a man yesterday morning. He called him Graham." I gave them a description.

Finn rubbed his chin. "That sounds like Graham Field. His farm is next to Donigal's."

"Have you told Bellamy?" Carina asked.

"Not yet. I figured he'd have a lot of people to interview, but I'll let him know." I wrote down the new info next to Graham's name. "I suppose we need to find out what they were arguing about."

Finnegan sat up straight and looked at me. "Do you think we could go and talk to him?"

"I don't see why not. It works in our favour that Bellamy hasn't gotten to him yet. He won't be on guard so much. What kind of person is he?"

"See, d'at's where it gets tough." Carina frowned. "He's not the friendliest of people, Avery. I heard rumours d'at he spent time in prison before he came here."

"How long ago was that?"

Finnegan answered, "About twelve years ago... a fair bit before Carina came here. I could look him up, see if he did. Find out why."

The plot thickened. "Can you do that before we interview him? I reckon, if you can get that done this morning, we can ambush him after lunch. He'd probably be working on his farm, right?"

He nodded slowly. "And we could have a quick look around before announcing ourselves."

I smiled. "We could."

Carina looked between Finn and me. "Don't go getting yourselves in trouble, now. He could be dangerous."

Finn patted her hand. "It'll be fine. I'm a strapping young dude, and Avery knows martial arts. Besides, Graham's an old guy."

"Yeah, but he has a shotgun. All farmers do."

Carina made a good point. "Don't worry. We'll be careful.

I can act all ditzy, and Vinegar can pretend he's mentoring me on the job. We can say it's practice."

Finn smirked. "Well, that is the truth."

I gave him a withering look. "You're such a d—"

"Hey, crew." MacPherson marched through the door exuding his usual enthusiastic energy. "Look at you three, hanging out together. What's the occasion?"

I wasn't going to answer that. I'd leave it up to one of the other two since they'd been here longer. Besides, I didn't care if MacPherson knew I was investigating this. Finn might want to hide it for some weird reason I couldn't fathom.

"Avery's just telling us about her first video interview for the company." Finn smiled.

"Good-oh." MacPherson looked at me. "As I texted you yesterday, great interview, Winters. You're a natural on camera. I wouldn't be averse to getting you to do some more. We're getting lots of hits on the net, and quite a few... comments."

I raised a brow because I could imagine the comments. "Unless they're comments giving information to the police, then I don't want to know." It would be easy to let the compliments get to my head, and all too easy to let the negative comments cut me down. I didn't want to deal with that emotional rollercoaster. I was better off not knowing or caring what strangers thought about my looks or interviewing skills.

"They're mostly positive, but you look professional, and you're representing us well. Keep it up. Based on how many visitors your interview brings, you'll get a bonus." Why hadn't he mentioned that before? I could become the queen of being on camera if *bonii* were on offer. He looked at Carina. "Mrs Viries called. They've asked if you wanted to join them for lunch before you do the interview with the club. I said you would. I hope that's okay. I'll never hear the end of it if you decline."

Carina shot a quick look at me and Finn. Reluctance leeched from her face. "Okay. I'll go." She packed her things up. "See you later. I expect a full update. Why don't we catch up at the pub tonight for a bite to eat? Around six?"

I shrugged. It was better than eating alone, and I could order an entrée, then have a sandwich at home. I'd promised Meg that money for tomorrow night, so if I wasn't careful, there'd be no money to save at the end of the week. Not that one week would hurt, but one week could turn into two, then three, etc., till I didn't save anything and found myself with no safety net. "Yep. Sounds good."

"I'll third that," said Finn. Carina and MacPherson left. Finnegan stared at me. How were his eyes so blue? They were probably the most mesmerizing deep sky blue I'd ever seen, and against his jet-black hair, it was striking.

I shook my head and cleared my throat, forcing my gaze to the window. *Get a grip, idiot.* Damn him and his effect on me. When I'd composed myself enough that I was pretty sure my tongue wasn't hanging out, I looked at him. His gaze hadn't shifted but his mouth had… into a smirk. Common-sense-stealing vulture. He knew exactly what he was doing, which was making me uncomfortable. He wasn't flirting. He was trying to get me under his spell. If I didn't resist, I'd be doing his laundry and cooking before I knew it and handing him my stories. "I have an appointment to get to. What time do you want to crash the farm?"

He looked at his phone. "It's just after ten, and I have a few things to do. What about two? I can meet you back here, and I'll drive us."

"Sure. Sounds like a plan." I rolled myself back to my desk

Carina style, pushing my feet against the floor and propelling myself like a champion. This was fun. "We should have a race one day—you, me, and Carina."

"What does the winner get?"

"I don't know. I'd have to think about it. Although, I shouldn't worry because I'm going to win." I waggled my brows as I reached my desk.

"Pfft, I'll leave you and Carina in my dust, Lightning. No doubt about it."

I stood and put my notebook in my bag. I hadn't unpacked anything else, so I was good to go. I'd taken to putting everything in a small backpack because then I didn't have to carry an extra laptop bag. It also meant I could pack a decent-sized bottle of water since I was walking so much. I only used Daisy when the walk was longer than fifteen minutes or it was raining heavily. "Yeah, yeah, you tell yourself that if it makes you feel better. I'll see you back here later. Ta-ta." I waved as I hurried out the door, not giving him time for a smarty-pants reply.

On my walk to Carly Wilson's house, I did my best to forget how flustered Finn made me. Holding his stare was almost painful—because the attraction was off the charts and I had to remind myself not to jump on him, and because he was only teasing me. His stomach wasn't flipping and flipping to the point of nausea. It was just a big joke to him. I wouldn't hate him for it though—he was just doing what he'd always done to get everyone's help or attention. It wasn't his fault that women responded that way.

My thoughts turned to Carly Wilson. She was a twenty-year-old student who was also a showjumper. She'd won some competition last week, which was the reason we were featuring her. I'd always admired people who could ride horses well.

They were large beasts who had a mind of their own. If they wanted you off, it was a long way to fall. Add to that flying through the air, and I was out. I had no idea how they held on when they landed. I'd been horse riding a few times, but I was as amateur as you could get.

She lived with her parents on a semi-rural property of two acres. Their house was a brick bungalow surrounded by lawn and a plethora of rose bushes, which were in full bloom. The fragrance was like running the gauntlet at a department store when all the salesladies wanted to spray you with their perfumes. I sneezed and rang the bell.

Heavy pounding came from inside, as if an actual horse was coming to answer the door. Did she ride her horse all the time? I was about to find out.

The door opened, and a young woman stood there, about my height, her red hair in a braid. A cute smattering of freckles decorated her long nose. She smiled. "Hello. You must be Avery. I'm Carly." She held her hand out for me to shake. Then she whinnied. Say what?

I was too busy shaking her hand to control my face, and my mouth dropped open. She'd ambushed me. Was it a joke? Was I supposed to laugh, or was she a weirdo? I looked into her eyes, and she seemed serious. Ooookay. I shut my mouth without laughing.

"Come out the back. I thought we could do the interview there, and then I can show you some showjumping. Will you put some photos in the paper?"

I smiled. "Yes, of course. I'm really looking forward to watching you jump. It's amazing what you horse people can do."

She snorted and tossed her head. "Thank you. Come this way." She turned around and bent at the waist, putting her hands on the ground so her hips were higher than her shoulders. Then she trotted down the hallway.

No. Freaking. Way. Was she the horse? I stayed where I was for a moment, stunned. This was next-level unusual. Ian, the tree lover, was normal compared to this. I shook my head and followed where she'd gone—through a door at the end of the hall.

We ended up going through a living area and out to a covered patio. She stopped and stood. "We can sit while we chat, and then I'll show you what I can do." One foot pawed at the ground. Well, she was raring to go.

My smile was fake—it was taking me a while to process the situation—but I hoped she didn't notice. It was the best I could do. "Sounds good." I sat in one of the outdoor wicker chairs, and she sat in the other. I took out my notebook. "So, how long have you been...."

"A horse?"

"Mmhmm. Yes." Right, not *behaving* like a horse. She thought she *was* a horse. For a judgemental person, this was turning out to be the wrong job. How was I meant to keep a straight face throughout this whole interview? I stared at the ground for a moment, searching for composure. My lip-twitching under control, I looked up.

"Ever since I can remember."

"And what kind of horse are you?" I added that to the list of questions I never thought I'd ever ask anybody.

"I'm an Arabian." She shook her head in a cross between a supermodel flicking her hair and, dare I say it, a horse shaking its mane.

"Hello. I'm Serina, Carly's mum." A slender woman, who had striking similarities to her daughter, came through the door carrying a tray. It held a pot of tea, one cup, a small milk jug, dish of sugar cubes, a small plate of biscuits, and a shallow plastic container without a lid. The contents of the container appeared to be chopped-up carrots. "I thought you might be a little peckish." She smiled and placed the tray on the low table between our chairs. She lifted the plastic container off the tray and went to the kitchen window. There were hooks coming out of the brickwork just under the window at chest height. She attached the container to them. Carly got out of her chair and went to the window.

My eyes widened. *No way!* I shook my head. *Yes way.*

Carly bent slightly and shoved her face into the container. Her mother patted her back. "Good girl." Carly neighed, and Serina turned to me. "When Carly's done, would you mind giving her a treat?"

What? "Um…"

She chuckled. "Silly me. See those sugar cubes. She's allowed to have two. Have you ever fed a horse?"

I couldn't say I had. And even if I had, how was that relevant? "No."

"Just hold your palm flat, like this." She demonstrated. "And put the cubes on it. That way, she won't accidentally bite you."

"Okay." I was totally washing my hands after this, and if they asked me to groom her, I was out.

"If you need anything else, let me know."

"Ah, thanks. Will do." Wow, she must really love her daughter. This was clearly a case of doing everything to keep her happy. I grabbed a biscuit while I waited for Carly to finish her food. Might as well enjoy the chocolate-chip goodness. I'd earned it. I took a bite and chewed. Then stopped midchew. Did Carly crap on the ground, or did she use a toilet? I was totally going to ask her. Stuff it. This was ridiculous, and if I had to endure it, I was going to ask whatever I wanted.

I didn't bother pouring tea, which I felt guilty for. She'd gone to all the trouble to make it, but I didn't feel like it. Old Avery would've done the polite thing, but I was working on being true to myself and not going against what I needed or wanted just to make other people happy. Sometimes it was important to push your needs aside to help someone else, but this wasn't that time. It was just a cup of tea. And I wasn't drinking it.

Finally, Miss Equine 2021 returned to her chair. "Can I ask you some more questions?" I mean, I had enough for an article just from observing, but it was probably better I didn't write it all from my... bemused point of view.

"Of course. Go ahead." She did that head-shake thing again.

"When did you get into showjumping?"

"Two years ago, I realised I had an aptitude for it. I really love it. There are quite a few events across the UK. I've competed in three already this year."

"How many people usually compete?" Surely there couldn't be that many horse people out there.

"There are four mares. We have our own competition. There's another one for stallions and geldings."

I choked on my own spit. When I was done coughing, I said, "Geldings?"

"They don't specify what they are. There's five who compete in that one." Her gaze strayed to the table. I was hoping she wouldn't want a treat until after I was gone. She looked at me. "Can you feed me my treat now? Sugar cubes are my favourite."

"I can. Do you mind if I photograph it? I'm sure our readers will want to know everything about your life."

She whinnied and nodded slowly, tipping her head as far back as it would go, then throwing it forward. "Yes. That's great."

I had a folded tripod in my bag, just in case. I fished it out and set it up, then put my phone on there. Filming would be the best way to go because I could get a still image from that later. Also, I was totally showing this to Meg and Carina. I'd already had to hold my tongue on the nude paintings, but honestly, I wasn't a saint, and my self-control only went so far.

I pressed Record, then grabbed the sugar cubes. This was going to be gross. "Do you want both at once?"

"One at a time, please."

I sat again and took one of the white cubes out of the dish and put it on my flat palm. Why me? I reached my hand out, and she leaned forward, her lips connecting with my palm. While she wasn't looking at me, it was safe to pull an "ew" face. Her lips tickled my skin, and I shuddered. This was worse than being touched by a ghost. I quickly put the other cube there, and she snaffled that up too. I wiped my hand on my cargo shorts—I'd dressed down today, knowing I was going to be walking and seeing horses. Horses my a—

She whinnied again. "Thank you. That was lovely."

"So, how did you feel when you won the showjumping?" I pressed Stop on the video, returned to my seat, and picked up my notebook and pen.

"I was so excited! It's been so much hard work to get good. I was the only one who managed the highest jump. I'm thinking of trying dressage soon." She stared off into the distance as if imaging herself high kneeing it across the arena.

Eventually, she came back to me. "Can I run through the course now?"

"I've been… looking forward to it." The course was set up on their vast, level lawn. Eight jumps in all—poles in the ground with bars across, fairly low. They reminded me of limbo bars. I was definitely filming this. We'd get thousands of hits for sure. This was a worldwide curiosity rather than just local. "Equine girl" had a nice ring to it. Despite the "I'm a horse" thing, she was athletic. "Does it hurt your hips or back doing that all the time?" It really didn't look comfortable.

"You get used to it." She made her way to her starting point, and I grabbed my phone.

I took a photo of her on all fours at the starting point. Once we were done, she took off. Her leaps from that position were impressive. Landing on her hands from a height made me cringe—that was an injury waiting to happen. But she completed the course with no dramas. Breathing heavily, she trotted to me and looked up but didn't say anything. I stared down at her. Well, this was awkward. She nudged my leg with her head. My gaze pinged around the yard, seeking a hint of what I was supposed to do. There it was again—nudge. The only thing I could think to do was pat her head. So I did.

I seriously did not get paid enough.

Patting her must've been the right thing to do because she walked off—on all fours—back to the patio.

I followed her. "Do you have your winning ribbon? I'd like to get a photo of you with that to finish up."

At the back door, she turned to me. "I'll get it. Just a sec."

When she returned, I got her to stand next to one of the jumps again. She did it on all fours…. "Smile." The photo done, I had one last question. "So, do you use a toilet, or do you go in the yard?"

"Done." I pressed Send on the email to MacPherson. It contained the article—"Horsing Around: Manesbury Mare Wins Showjumping Championship"—and a link to the videos I'd taken. I'd gone home for lunch, then come in. It took me just over an hour to write the article. Even though it wasn't long, I needed to be careful my humour was subtle—I didn't want to upset Carly, but there was a fine line because how could it not be an article on the ridiculous? I didn't care what anyone said—if you couldn't laugh at someone living life as a horse, what could you laugh at?

Finn came in shortly after that, but he didn't bother going to his desk. He stopped at mine and looked down at me. "Ready to go?"

"I guess so. I'll just pack my stuff up."

"Have you got an umbrella? It looks like it's going to rain."

"Yep. Always. My motto with your weather is to expect the unexpected." I chuckled. Not that I always used umbrellas because I was trying to avoid being hit by lightning a second time, but if it was rain and none of the storm theatrics, I'd use it.

"You're not wrong."

Within a couple of minutes, we were getting into his car. He started the engine, then turned to me. "So, what's the plan?"

I stared at him. "I thought you'd have one? What happened to the 'I'm showing Avery the ropes' idea?"

He smiled. "Leaving it up to you. You seem capable, and since I'm not supposed to be doing anything with this one, if anything happens, I can say it's your idea."

"Gee, thanks." As he pulled into the street, I said, "I figure we go there and just ask if he's seen him, you know, kind of like we're just door knocking. We can ask a few questions, and at the end, I can pretend that I've realised all of a sudden that I saw him in the village, and then go, ooh, that's right, you were arguing with Mr Donigal."

He nodded, appreciation on his face. "I like it. Good thinking, Lightning. Have you got any other info?"

"Not at the moment." Charles still hadn't gotten back to me. I'd tried calling him at lunch, but he didn't respond. Hopefully he was in the middle of getting some good intel. "I'm hoping to have more to tell you guys at dinner. And maybe talking to Graham today will help shake something else loose. Did you find out why he was in prison?"

"Nope. Couldn't find anything." He flicked his gaze to me before looking back at the road. "I'm wondering if he's changed his name. There was absolutely no information about him with that name. I found a few other Graham Fields, but they were all the wrong age or location, and none of them had been incarcerated."

"Hmm, so what's he hiding?" I tapped my finger on the door and eyed the darkening sky, a flutter of worry vibrating my chest.

"That's what we're going to discover." Finn's confidence in our abilities was comforting, but was it misguided? We were about to find out.

# CHAPTER 7

Entry to Graham's farm was via a timber and metal gate that was chained to a thick timber pole concreted into the ground. There was no intercom, and the house wasn't visible from the road. An expanse of rolling hills fell away from where we stood in front of the car. Sheep grazed, and birds soared overhead under the heavy sky. The view over the district was pretty—if not darkened by the coming storm—Manesbury village was a smattering of grey and orange roofs. A shaft of hazy light broke through the clouds and spotlighted one of the fields. Nature was always putting on a show. Unfortunately, fear tempered my appreciation. A storm meant thunder and lightning. Because I didn't want to be a burden—or be made fun of—I schooled my features into what I hoped was calmness. "So, now what?"

Finn shook the gate again, confirming it was indeed locked. "How do you feel about jumping fences?"

Again, thank you, sensible clothes. "I'm always up for jumping fences, especially when I'm wearing cargo pants." I ignored the drop of rain that splatted on my cheek. "I'll take my phone. We can record everything rather than write it down. If we have to run, I'd rather not be carrying a heap of stuff."

"Good idea. We might also need to call for help. I'll take mine too." Hmm, thanks for the reminder that he might be an ex-prison dweller. He gave me a reassuring look. "But don't worry. I won't let anything happen to you."

*Swoon.* Not that he wanted to protect me because he was into me, but still. At least he didn't dislike me and want to leave me to die. Not that anyone was going to die here today, but whatever. "Thanks. I appreciate it." I grinned. I didn't bother reminding him I had martial-arts skills. They probably wouldn't be very useful against a gun at distance. Graham was old and slender enough that I could take him out if I had to. There was no way he'd be as fast as me either. If worst came to worst, I'd run.

I grabbed my phone out of my bag. Finn grabbed his mobile and an umbrella and locked the car. "Need any help over the gate?"

"Nah, I'm good, but thanks."

He watched and waited for me to go first, probably in case I had no idea about my abilities and needed help. I rolled my eyes as I climbed up and over, landing safely on the other side. "Piece of cake." Once he was over, we followed the driveway, and I started filming—you never knew when you'd need the information.

As we walked, the rain went from a drop here and there to a light drizzle. Perfect. At least it wasn't freezing. It was in the mid-twenties, which was warm for England. Finn put up his umbrella and sidled up next to me. "Here. We can share."

My heart raced, and not because Finn was next to me.

"Ah, no thanks. You're a walking lightning rod with that up here." I panned my gaze over the grassy hill that only had a couple of trees. "You're one of the highest points out here."

"They say lightning never strikes twice, so I figure I'm safer if I'm next to you."

"Ha ha, it can strike twice, and I certainly can too." I lightly jabbed him in the side a couple of times.

"Hey! Stop beating me up." He protected his side with one arm and gave me a mock-hurt look.

"Step away from me with that umbrella. I'd rather be wet."

"You're for real?"

"Yes." I hurried along the dirt driveway, cringing at all the drops pattering annoyingly on my face. After a minute or so, we reached the top of the hill, which flattened and revealed Graham's two-storey brick home with attached triple garage about a hundred and fifty metres away. Like Donigal's farm, there was a large shed that likely housed tractors and other machinery. There were no stables though. A fence line ran either of the driveway and behind the house. The land then divided into various paddocks. One had a rich green crop, a couple had sheep, and the others just looked like grass. He probably rotated his sheep in different areas.

"Looks like he's here." Finnegan gave a nod towards a white van parked in front of the garage.

Thunder echoed from a fair distance away, but my hackles still raised. I swallowed. "Yeah. Um. Let's see if he has any video security. If not, we can have a look in the shed before we knock on the door."

"Good call."

As we made our way to the shed, I put a shielding hand on my forehead to protect my eyes and checked out the sky. It didn't look promising. "If Graham says anything about us going into the shed, I'll tell him I was scared by the storm." Would Finnegan see the truth in that statement?

"Ha, good excuse. You're so good at this."

"I'm taking that as a compliment." He could've meant that I was good at deception.

He grinned. "Well, it's a good quality in a journalist but maybe not so much in a girlfriend."

*Hmm, thanks for confirming you'd hate to date me....* Good thing I didn't need him or any other man.

The thunder rumbled again, closer this time. I jogged the rest of the way to the vast shed. A quick look at the outside confirmed there were no security cameras. I opened the door and ducked inside. Rain pinged off the roof, sounding heavier in here than it actually was.

An oily stench slicked the inside of my nostrils—a tractor, motorbike, old lathe, and classic Jaguar with the hood open were the likely suspects. It was hard to pick out more details in the dim interior. Finn came inside and shut the door. He flicked a light on. "That's better." He put his hands on his hips and gazed around.

I remembered I was still filming, so I held my phone up and panned it around. If there was anything out of place, I couldn't see it. I walked around and filmed in every nook and cranny. Hmm. I made sure to film the number plate of the old car. Maybe we could find out more information about his past life by looking up the registration or old sales details. They must be recorded somewhere. It certainly wouldn't hurt.

"Is this blood?" Finn was standing next to a workbench that sat along one wall, tools covering its surface.

I joined him and peered at a vice attached to the side of the bench. "Damn. We should've brought something to take a sample. It could be paint for all we know." I took a close-up of it anyway.

Finn turned his head. "Here we go." He reached over and picked up a small plastic bag and a screwdriver sitting amongst the crowd of tools, screws, and offcuts of timber on the bench, then scraped some of the rusty-red substance into the bag. He slid the small pouch into his pocket and put the screwdriver back. "It's probably nothing, but you never know."

The slow pitter-patter of rain became a deafening stampede. Thunder cracked overhead, and the windows rattled. I dropped to the floor and crawled under the workbench. Cobwebs caught in my hair and face, but that was preferable to being out in the open—even though we were inside, it felt like being out there. I sat with my knees pulled to my chest, arms around them. *Concentrate on your breathing.* I counted as I breathed in, then out, making sure I breathed for four seconds for each inhale, then again for every exhale.

I shut my eyes and willed the storm to go away.

"Avery, are you all right?" I sensed a body in front of me. "Avery?"

The masculine freshness of Finnegan's deodorant filled my nostrils, and I opened my eyes. He was staring at me with concern on his face. "Do you have PTSD from the lightning strike?"

I hated admitting weakness, but it was impossible to deny, so why waste the energy? "Yes." I took another deep breath, fighting the panic that wanted me to curl in a ball and shut down.

"Look at me." He touched the top of my knee and stared into my eyes. "What colour are my eyes?"

"Blue."

"Like a sunny sky. Now, shut your eyes and imagine a

sunny day." I did as he said. "Now, imagine you're walking along the seaside at Brighton."

Despite the terror clawing at the edges of my resolve, a small smile pushed its way onto my face. Trust him to come up with something I had no idea about. "I've never been. What does it look like?"

"There's rows and rows of old houses and apartments opposite the aqua water. The beach is made up of gazillions of pebbles, and long wharfs jut out into the sea. Large gulls glide around and cry out to each other. When they land, it's to con chips from whomever they can."

Thunder boomed again. I started and scrunched my eyes shut even tighter. At least it was a rumble rather than a crack. The storm must be moving away, slowly.

"It's okay, Avery. I'm here. You're going to be fine. The storm's blowing over, and soon we'll go and interview Graham." He put a warm hand on my knee, and I focussed on it, blocking out everything else. I hated that I was cowering under a table and shutting down. I was an adult, not a child, for goodness' sake. As the storm's grumblings faded into the distance, my cheeks heated. So embarrassing.

I opened my eyes and met Finn's assessing gaze. "Sorry." I shook my head. "It's ridiculous, I know, but I can't control it. My body has a mind of its own, and it's not my mind." Give me a person to fight, and I'd step up, but nature… that was another story.

He kept his hand where it was for a moment, and as much as I hated to admit it, it was nice. "It's not your fault. Don't beat yourself up. I'm not saying don't work on it, but give yourself a break. Being hit by lightning is major. You're allowed to be freaked out." He squeezed my knee—sending my heart, which had calmed down somewhat, racing again—and let go. "You good to come out from under there?"

I mentally checked in with myself. "Yes. Sorry." He looked at me as if to say, don't say sorry! And I almost apologised for saying sorry. I chuckled instead. "Okay, I won't say sorry or sorry for saying sorry."

He grinned. "That's more like it." He backed out from under the bench and stood.

I followed and dusted myself down, patting off years of accumulated dust and bug carcasses. "Thanks for helping me. It… helped." I gave him a closed-mouth smile. My brain wasn't quite working properly again, so he'd have to forgive me the repetition. As a journalist, I was always paranoid about using the same words over and over, and it came through in my speech too. Man, being me was hard work.

He returned my smile. "I'm happy to know my help helped." His head fell back, and he stared at the iron roof. "Sounds like the rain's easing as well. Let's get our bums to the house and hope he'll talk to us."

"Okay." To show him that I wasn't going to freak out again, I was the first to the door. I opened it. Looking out, I ignored the anxiety-fuelled metallic taste in my mouth. Lightning flashed in the distance, but this hilltop was safe. I pushed the door all the way open and jogged towards the house—there was no point dawdling and getting drenched.

The veranda ran half the length of the home. It was nice to get out of the weather. Pretending to myself that we were just here trying to help find Mr Donigal rather than sussing out Graham, I relaxed my shoulders and knocked loudly. If I believed it, he would too, right?

Finn stood next to me just as the door opened. Graham

stood there in a holey T-shirt and long shorts. "What do you want? You're trespassing." Well, that could've gone better.

"We're from the *Manesbury Daily*, but we're not here for a story. V— Finnegan here"—I turned and nodded at him—"has a friend who's been arrested in relation to Mr Donigal going missing. We wanted to talk to you since you're his neighbour. We don't think Finnegan's friend did it, and we wondered if you heard anything last night or knew of anyone who might have had it in for Mr Donigal."

Lips pressed together, he looked from me to Finn, then back. "I didn't hear or see anything. I was asleep. I go to bed at eight every night, get up at four thirty. Farm work starts early."

"Did you know him well?" *Argh, please give us something.*

"I've spoken to him a few times over the years, obviously—we are neighbours—but we didn't sit and have tea together. I keep to myself."

"So, you don't know anyone who would've had a problem with him?"

"No."

"When was the last time you spoke to him?"

"I can't remember. Now, if you can please get off my property, I'd appreciate it." He shut the door.

Right.

Argh, what a waste of time, and why was I so bad at getting information from him? I turned to Finn, who was frowning. There was more on the line for him than me. I really had no idea whether Alfie had anything to do with Donigal going missing, but it was my duty to find out. I hated the idea of an innocent person going to prison. "Maybe you should've asked the questions. He might not respect women. I think we made a big mistake." He certainly looked old school, and he kept to himself generally, but he was also a liar. I'd seen him yesterday arguing with Donigal. The more I thought about it, the angrier I got. Stuff it.

"Well, it's too late now. Let's just get going. We tried." He turned, but I grabbed his arm.

"No, it's not. I'm going to try something else first, something he'll understand more than a polite woman." I jammed my teeth together and faced the door. I banged on it as hard as I could. I was sick of being ignored, underestimated, discounted, lied to. I might not get what I wanted, but I was bloody well going to try harder before I let people win.

The door flew open, and Graham stood there, one hand in a fist at his side. His eyes shot sparks. "I thought I told you to leave."

"Not until you give us some information. I saw you arguing in the village with Donigal yesterday morning. I also know that Graham Field isn't your real name. Would you like me to tell the police about your argument yesterday? Would you like them to drag you in there for questioning?" I ignored the faint intake of breath behind me. The urge to smile at taking Finn by surprise was strong, but now wasn't the time, so I folded my arms and stared the old man down.

He narrowed his eyes, the wrinkles at their corners deepening into chasms. "No one threatens me, girlie."

I shrugged. "Have it your way. I guess you can expect to be down at the police station this afternoon. It's interesting that you won't help us. Maybe you do have something to hide." I was figuring the something to hide was related to his past rather than Mr Donigal going missing, but you never knew.

He swore. "Fine. If I tell you what I know, will you keep what you saw to yourself?"

This was another time that my looks played in my favour. No one would assume a sweet-looking young woman would lie. My face was as earnest as all get out. And yes, I saw the irony here. I hated that he'd lied to us, but he was trying to hide something. I was trying to find it. "I will." I was the only one who answered, which was good because if I thought he did it after what he had to say, Finn could try and find someone else who'd seen the altercation and then tell the police. Or Finn could tell Bellamy I said something about it, so technically it wouldn't be me saying anything. Yes, it was the faintest line ever, but there was no way my word to a murderer was more important than that murderer going to prison.

"Last year, we had to repair one of the boundary fences. We both did the work, but with materials, it was still six thousand pounds. He still owes me half and refuses to pay. And now he's missing, I probably won't ever see that money, so it's in my best interests for him to turn up alive." He folded his arms.

"Won't you be able to claim it from his estate?" Finn asked.

"I don't want to get involved in a legal thing. I don't have the money to spare."

That seemed fair enough, or did it? Maybe he didn't want to draw attention to himself. "Is there anyone else he owes money to that you know of?"

"You might want to talk to the farm supply store in Cramptonbury—Furl and Sons. That's all I'm saying. I'm done." He stepped back and shut the door.

Finn looked at me. "Interesting."

"Very. I suppose we should get out of here."

"Agreed."

The rain had slowed to a light drizzle. We jogged back to the car on what was now a muddy driveway. Gumboots would've been good. My sneakers were a filthy catastrophe. When we reached the car, Finn looked at both our shoes. He went to the boot and pulled out a plastic bag. "Gotta be prepared in a country of persistent rain." He opened my door. "Sit, take your shoes off, and put them in here."

I did as asked. When I was done, he went around the driver's side and did the same with his shoes. When the plastic bag was safely in the back seat, we were off. I wasn't sure if the information I'd forced out of Graham would lead to anything, but at least we'd gotten something. "So, do you feel like taking a trip to Furl and Sons?"

Finn smiled. "Is the Pope Catholic?" He glanced at me. "Nice work back there, by the way. Remind me never to get on your bad side."

I smirked. "How do you know you're not already on it?"

He chuckled. "Touché." His mirth dribbled away. "I wanted to say thank you for helping. I appreciate it."

I almost made a joke about how much and would he give me info from Bellamy if I asked in the future, but that wasn't right when he was so concerned about his friend. It was a terrible predicament to be in. "It's my pleasure. I like getting to the bottom of things. I'm sorry to ask, but what if he did do it?"

He took a deep breath, then sighed. "I don't know. I haven't thought that far ahead because I can't believe he'd do anything like that. Sometimes you just have to have faith."

Finn was a smart guy, and even though we could be blind to our friends' or loved-ones' faults, I gave him the benefit of the doubt. For now, I'd fight as hard as I could to get to the bottom of it. Even if Alfie was guilty, at least Finn would be able to have closure. Either way, it was important.

The rest of the fifteen-minute trip consisted of silence or small talk. I was reluctant to ask him too many questions about himself because I didn't want him to think I was interested in him, and maybe he was a bit scared of me after seeing me have a storm-induced meltdown. Awkward.

Before we got out of the car, I looked at Finn. "I think we'll need a plan. They're not going to give out confidential information to just anyone. He's got a son, right? Maybe you could pretend to be him and say you're chasing up your father's debts because he's missing, and your mother asked you to?"

"And why are you with me?"

"I'm your lawyer and I'm looking into it as well."

"You look a bit young to be a lawyer. If I didn't know you were twenty-five, I'd think you were like nineteen or twenty."

I wrinkled my brow. "How do you know how old I am?"

"Julian showed me your resume. He asked me to help him choose from all the different candidates. He didn't tell me who he picked until I met you though."

Dare I ask if Finn picked me or someone else? Yeah, nah. I didn't need that in my head either—that he'd rejected me in the first place. At the end of the day, out of all the candidates, MacPherson picked me. I should be proud because there'd probably been quite a few applicants. "Oh, okay. So, what do you think about the idea?"

"I think you can just be my girlfriend, offering support."

"I guess I can just look pretty and say nothing." I conjured my most sarcastic expression.

"Yep." He gave me a sexy grin and pulled the bag from the bag seat. He was so trying to rile me up. Stupid man. It was working.

I opened my door, swung my legs out, and put my shoes on. When I hopped out of the car and shut my door, it wasn't loudly at all. I wasn't that immature. Well, not most of the time.

He waited for me to catch up to him before he went inside the single-level warehouse-style brick building. The faint gag-inducing tang of fertiliser hit my nostrils first, followed by a richer hay odour. We walked down an aisle of all manner of gardening tools, wheelbarrows, and even a ride-on mower. Finn looked at the mower wistfully as we passed.

"I didn't pick you for a ride-on-mower kind of guy." He did have a lawn, but I'd seen the lawn-chomping goats that did our lawns next door too. He didn't need to mow.

"What guy isn't a ride-on-mower kind of guy?"

Okay, so I couldn't argue with that. Brad even mentioned wanting one once. When I pointed out we lived in a unit, he said maybe we should look at getting a house in the country. I'd rolled my eyes because he was not a country person—he was scared of spiders and moths for a start, and the only manual labour he'd ever done in his life was.... Huh. I couldn't even remember. "Fair point."

We found a service desk at the back of the place, and Finn asked to speak to the manager. The young lady batted her eyelashes before going off to get the manager. I couldn't help it, and I rolled my eyes. Finn looked at me. "What?"

"Nothing." I batted my lashes and gave him a fake closed-mouth smile.

"Can I help you?" The manager was a fit-looking male in his forties. He wore a black apron over his fawn-coloured shirt and workman's trousers.

Finn held his hand out. "Hi. I'm Albert Donigal, and I understand my father has an account with you that might be overdue." From my research, I knew he had a son, but I was sure his name was Danny. Although if Danny had been here before, they would know what he looked like, so maybe Finn was onto something. And it was nice to see I wasn't the only liar on the block.

Tom—according to his name tag—shook Finn's hand. "Well, this is unexpected. Yes, we have an account for your father, but we'll need authorization from him in order to speak to you."

I sucked in a breath and grabbed Finn's arm. I stared at him as if waiting for disaster. He blinked, and he appeared to be figuring out how to respond. He finally said, "My father's missing, hence my visit. We're not sure what's happened. He might be d-dead." Finn's shoulders drooped.

"It's okay, sweetie." I rubbed his back. This girlfriend stuff was hard work.

Tom's mouth dropped open. "I—I'm so sorry."

Finn was pretending he was trying not to cry, so I butted in. "That's why we're here. His mother's beside herself with worry, and she wanted to know what was happening with the farm accounts. She normally has nothing to do with it, and Albert's brother, Danny, is too busy with the police and trying to find their father that Albert decided to come in."

"I'm so sorry. I'll get the iPad. Just a moment."

Finn squeezed my hand and whispered, "Nice work."

I ignored the tingles fanning up my arm. "Of course—I'm a professional." The heat from his hand was rather distracting, and I wanted to let go, but if I was playing the supportive girl-friend, it would probably look weird, and funnily enough, he wasn't letting go either.

Tom returned, iPad in hand, a document on the screen. "This is what your father owes. He's three months behind." He turned the screen our way.

Holy moly begoly. Donigal owed over fourteen thousand pounds. Fertiliser, insecticide, and hay were expensive. Finn shook his head. "Right. Can you print me out a copy of that, and I'll make sure it gets paid ASAP?"

"I know you're in difficult circumstances, but can you pay some of it today?" Tom leaned back slightly, as if expecting an explosion.

Finn swallowed and sighed. He took a deep, shuddering breath. His acting skills were better than mine. I'd have to remember that for the future. "Could you print that out, please? I'll show my mum tonight, and I'll help her transfer some of it. Would that be okay?"

Tom cocked his head to the side. "Could you transfer 20 per cent today and the rest next week?" Tom was trying to be fair, and the bill was overdue by quite a bit. He was actually dealing with this in a very understanding way. Now I felt horrible that he wasn't going to get his money this afternoon.

"Yes, of course." When Tom went to print the receipt, Finn leaned near my ear and whispered, "Now I feel like a numpty."

Damn breath on my neck making me shiver. The sooner we got out of here, the better. "Me too." *Hurry up, Tom.* At this point, I had to assume Finn didn't realise the effect he had on me because he wouldn't want to encourage scary Avery's attention. That made me feel a bit better. I worried that my attraction was all over my face when I looked at him, as much as I tried to look nonplussed.

Tom strode out of the back office with a piece of paper in hand. "Here you go." He handed it to Finn. "Please let me know if there are any more problems. Our number's on the invoice."

Finn's smile looked grateful. "I will. Thank you so much for understanding."

As soon as we were out of the shop, I took my hand back.

We didn't speak till we got back in the car. I clicked my belt in. "So, Donigal had money problems."

Finn pulled out onto the road. "Looks that way. But Tom didn't look like he was out to get him. He seemed like a good guy, to be honest."

"Agreed, and I'm pretty sure we can discount him as a suspect, but he's helped us build a picture of the situation. If it wasn't Graham, maybe someone else wasn't as patient while waiting for his money."

The rest of the drive back was quiet. My thoughts oscillated between figuring out where to look next and the stomach-tingling sensation of Finn's breath on my neck and ear. A pox on him and his sexiness. He was probably thinking about his friend and maybe what he was going to have for dinner at the pub.

"Can you drop me at home? I have a couple of things I need to do before dinner."

"Yeah, sure."

As soon as I'd locked my door, I sat on the couch and called to Charles. Hopefully he wasn't still ignoring me. We could use some more info. Just as I was going to say his name for the second time, he appeared and sat next to me. "Hey."

"Hey, yourself. What have you been up to? It's been ages since your last update." When you were waiting on information, ten minutes could feel like ages, but twenty-four hours was legit a long time.

"Sorry. There's been a lot going on at the station. I lost track of time."

"Fair enough. So, tell me all the news." I took out my laptop and opened it on my lap. It was a shame I couldn't record this on my phone—technology hadn't updated to pick up ghosts yet. Luckily, my typing speed was a hundred and twenty-five words per minute, so it wouldn't be too hard to keep up with Charles.

He crossed his legs as if he was sitting on the ground. "They found Mr Donigal's watch at Alfie's house."

"What?! That's huge news. When did this happen? Why didn't you tell me straight away?"

"It was early this morning. Bellamy came in afterwards talking about it, then said he was going home for breakfast and some sleep. Said he'd be back in the office after lunch."

I put all that in the computer. "Have they interviewed anyone else?"

"After they found the watch, they got Mrs Donigal and her son to come in to confirm it was his. Bellamy told them where they were at with the investigation. They didn't say much. Oh, also, turns out the car was found outside one of Alfie's friends' houses. A young couple."

My eyes widened. "Oh, fresh cat vomit. That's not good. Have they interviewed them?"

"They have an alibi for the night Mr Donigal went missing, but they've been warned to stay in the area for the next few days in case the police have any more questions."

I blew out a breath. Finnegan was not going to be happy. "Anything else?"

"No, but I don't think Alfie did it. He's been so dejected, and he's even cried a couple of times when he's alone. He prayed out loud once, and from what he said, he doesn't believe he did it." He slid off the couch. "Sorry, but I have to go again. I need time in the ghost realm. I've never been in the living realm as much as I have since you got here, and it gets hard sometimes. I think I need to go back and kind of recharge. I'll see you when I see you." He faded away.

"Bye," I said to the empty room. Well, that was all new

information on the case and ghosts. It was interesting—and somewhat depressing—that you didn't suddenly become all-knowing when you died. Charles was still learning how to exist after being a ghost for decades.

So, we had two strong suspects—Graham and Alfie. I had to believe Donigal's ghost when he called his killer a "he." The owner of the pet-supply store wasn't a suspect as far as I could tell. Running a business, he probably had a fair few accounts go into the red, and if you killed everyone who did that, you'd be a serial killer. Also, Tom seemed like a decent guy. Not once while we were there did he look like he was going to lose his temper, and there was no crazy in his eyes.

I wrote up my thoughts in the notebook and considered how much to tell Finn and Carina. If I told them too much, they were going to wonder how in hades I'd gotten all that information. So, what mattered to us and what we were trying to achieve, and what didn't? Should we talk to Alfie's other friends? Come to think of it, Finn probably knew them if they were all friends with Alfie. Maybe I could mention that my source had seen them go into the police station, and he could call them himself. Then he could get that information, and it wouldn't look sus on my part.

Right. What else? Hmm, I might bring up the man who was there supporting the wife. Maybe he wanted to move in on his mate's woman? You never knew. We should at least look into the guy. Which brought me to motive. That was one. The other obvious one was that he owed money to someone who was sick of waiting. And, lastly, firing someone. But where was the body?

If only I could get back to the farm and talk to Donigal. From what Everly had once told me, new ghosts tended to gravitate to their home or place of death. If we knew where he was killed, the police would have an easier time finding the body, which would hopefully give them more clues. But then again, Charles had seen him lying in the barn. Had he been killed and hidden somewhere on his own farm? I was thinking maybe he was still alive when Charles had seen him, and he left there by himself and died later. Maybe he was taking himself to the hospital? Or maybe someone else took him away. Had his death been an accident and he'd died on the way to get help?

I sighed. Too many scenarios. How did the police figure this stuff out with minimal evidence? What a nightmare. They didn't even know for sure—like I did—that he was dead. Next time I spoke to Charles, I'd get him to do a flyover of Donigal's farm. Maybe there'd be a clue somewhere... or a body. It was better than chatting to Bellamy and asking if they'd searched the place. We were on good terms at the moment because I'd helped them solve the last murder case, and I was trying not to ruin that straight away.

Once my list was done, I had a shower and got ready for dinner. It would be nice to chat to Carina outside of work, and I'd be lying if I didn't admit to wanting to see Finn again, but that was bad. Very bad. At this rate, I'd be pathetically throwing myself at him or Bailey before the week was done. *I stared at the ceiling. No. You are not going to go there. It's not worth it. You're finally happy and peaceful... well, except for when your parents take pot shots from across the ocean.* I inhaled deeply and took control of myself. I wasn't helpless—I had a say in how I lived my life, and a few hormones weren't going to ruin what I wanted for myself.

Pep talk done, I walked to the pub.

I said hello to Bailey first and grabbed a drink, then joined Carina and Finn at the table. Meg was running around serving meals, so I just waved. As soon as I sat, Carina was into it. "What did you two find out today? I'm dying to know."

Finn told her about our visit to the farm and surprisingly left out the part about my panic attack. "You should've seen Avery go. She went straight for the jugular." He grinned.

Carina broke out a huge smile. "D'at doesn't surprise me. Our Avery's a champion for the trut'."

"Yeah, but I lie a fair bit to get the truth. Do the ends justify the means?" Guilt ate away at me sometimes— depending on who I was lying to—but not all the time. I obviously thought it was a valid way to get important information, but it would be good to know what they thought. Maybe they'd stop being friends with me when they realised how much I played hooky with the truth.

Carina gave me a piercing look. "D'ey definitely do. Lying to friends is different, but lying to uncover d'e trut'… you gotta do what you gotta do. Just don't lie to me, and we'll be good."

I smiled. "I won't. You're one of the only real friends I've had since I was in high school." I laughed nervously. "That's kind of embarrassing to admit to, but before I came here, I hung out with Brad and his friends… and they weren't mine. Anyway, it's all good. That life is far behind me." I pretended they weren't looking at me with sympathy. Argh, I sounded so pitiful. "Anyway, after the farm, we went to the farm-supply place, and he owes money there, like a lot of money, but that guy didn't seem like the killing kind."

"Agreed," said Finn. "I feel kind of bad lying to him though. He'll be waiting for his money, and it won't come."

"Maybe we should send the invoice to Mrs Donigal with a note, pretending it's from him. Maybe she'll be more willing to pay it?"

"But what if d'ey have no money?" Carina took a sip of her wine.

I shrugged. "Their house was what I'd call rundown. I don't think it's been renovated for fifty years. Everything was worn and tired, including Mrs Donigal. I guess living on a farm doesn't make for an easy life."

Finn leaned forward. "But Graham seems to think he has the money, and he's just stingy. We need to find out which it is."

"How are we supposed to do that?" Even if I told them about the finance guy the police had interviewed, there was no way he'd tell us confidential customer information.

"We can order a title register. It lists landowners and whether there's any mortgages. We can also order a title plan, which shows the boundaries. If that farm is as big as I think it is, it's worth a fortune. He could be sitting on two-and-a-half or three million pounds, depending how much land he has. There was talk of some of that area being redeveloped into large residential holdings. There was a protest about four years ago, but it's all gone quiet. In any case, he could easily sell, pay all his bills, move to a normal house, and live quite comfortably for the rest of his life, considering how old he is."

"Okay, well let's do that then. I'll check out the zonings at council." Hopefully they didn't remember me from last time when I caused a bit of a fuss… and probably had someone thrown in jail. Could they ban someone from the council?

"I tell you what, I have knitting club tomorrow night. Mrs Donigal doesn't go, but a couple of her friends do. I'll feel d'em out."

"Great idea." I smiled. With the three of us working this case, maybe we really could solve it.

"Hello!" Meg stood next to my chair. "What's everyone

having?" We all said hello and told her our orders. "Is this a work dinner?"

"Kind of," I said. "We're just trying to work out what happened to Mr Donigal."

"Oh, God, yes." She looked down at me. "You and Bailey were the last people to see him… well, and some of our other patrons." She shook her head. "I heard they arrested Alfie. I just can't believe he'd do something horrible."

Finn frowned. "You and me both."

"Change of subject, sorry. What are you guys doing tomorrow night? We're having a charity speed-dating night, and you have to come. We've got daters signed up from Cramptonbury and Shillington, but we're still short of our target in donations. It would be great if we could get maybe six more participants."

"Oh, what a screaming shame. I have plans." Carina did not sound like she thought it was a shame. Not even a little bit.

"I can't. Sorry."

She looked at Finn. "Why can't you? Dating's your thing, isn't it? You have to come. Please."

He smirked, then swung his devious gaze to me. "I'll go on one condition."

My eyes widened. "Oh, no you don't. I'm not going. I already told Meg."

Meg stared at me. "I haven't given up on you yet, missy. Please come. You'll be helping suicidal teens. That's a good cause, right?"

"And if you don't go, I'm not going. It's all on you." Finn's smiling eyes stayed pinned on me. I'd get him back one day.

Hmm, maybe I could write an article on it. Then I wouldn't totally be wasting my time. "I'll do it on one condition." I looked at Finn. "I get to write the story."

He narrowed his eyes. "Do you always have to have an angle?"

"Yes. The story is mine. Take it or leave it." I raised one eyebrow.

He rolled his eyes. Ha! He must've been planning on doing a piece on it. "Fine. You can have the story."

"Aw, isn't d'is lovely." Carina grinned. "Look how well you two are compromising."

I gave her a deadpan look and showed her my middle finger. It just made her laugh.

Meg clapped. "Great! Now that's decided, I'll fill in the sign-up sheet for you." Hmm, that was probably so neither of us could chicken out. "Your dinners will be out shortly." And with that, she turned and headed towards the kitchen.

I gave Finn a withering look. "Why did you have to go and do that? I'm not dating at the moment. It's literally the last thing I want to be doing."

"Pfft. You worry too much. It's what, five minutes talking to someone you'll never see again, multiplied by ten? Just be boring—which shouldn't be hard for you—and you'll have no worries about any of them wanting your number." He looked pretty pleased with himself.

"Great advice. I'll just talk about you. That should work." I smiled sweetly.

Carina leaned over and high-fived me. "Burn!"

Finn tried to look cranky, but he couldn't hold back the laughter. "I should know not to mess with an Aussie. You guys wrangle spiders, snakes, and drop bears. You call each other swear words as a form of endearment."

"We do. We're rough as guts—which is also one of my favourite sayings." Talking about Australia should've made me homesick, but it didn't. I had no one to be homesick for. Yes, I cared about my sister, but we didn't spend a lot of time together when I was there, so I didn't really miss her. Everyone else… well, they were the reason I was on the other side of the world.

"Now d'at's out of d'e way, what else do you have to tell us?" Carina was looking at me.

I reached into my handbag and took out my notebook. "Right, well…. My source said they saw a young couple get called in for questioning—Mr and Mrs Marlow. Apparently they're friends of Alfie's. Do either of you know them?"

Carina shook her head, but Finn leaned forward. "I do. What do they have to do with it?"

I shrugged. "I have no idea. Can you check it out, maybe? I'm sure if you gave them a call and said you heard they were allowed to visit Alfie and you wanted to know how he was doing, they might spill. If they're your friends and you asked them if they were questioned and why, they'd probably tell you without passing that on to Bellamy. I mean, surely he knows you're going to ask some questions. As long as you don't ask him anything or make trouble, I can't see how he can get upset with you."

"True. I'm going to call them now." He pushed his chair back and stood. "I'll be back in five." He headed outside—it was way too noisy in here to make a serious phone call.

Carina and I chatted about random stuff until Finn returned about ten minutes later, by which time our dinners had arrived. As he sat, I swallowed my mouthful. "So, what's the news? What did they say?"

He rubbed his forehead, as if he had a headache. "The police found Donigal's car in front of their house."

"Oh my lord!" Carina's mouth fell open. "D'at's major.

Ald'ough, it could be a coincidence. Did they find any trace of Donigal?"

"No. At least no body. But it doesn't look good for Alfie." He slouched in his chair and hung his head. Then he looked up again. "We need to figure this out. I still can't believe he'd do something bad to someone."

"It would be good to find out if there was any blood in the car. I have a feeling they should be looking for Donigal's body." That's as close as I'd get to saying I knew he was dead.

Carina's concerned gaze met mine. "Why do you t'ink d'at?"

"Just a feeling I have. The longer a person is missing, the worse the outcome, usually. His car had been hidden—it's not like he would hide his own car. Did they search your friends' house for evidence?"

"Yes. But they haven't found anything… yet." He looked forlornly at his dinner.

Carina patted his back. "Lost your appetite, Finny?"

"Yeah." He ran a hand through his raven hair and swigged his beer.

"We'll get to the bottom of it. Try not to worry." As much as we ribbed each other, and I was worried about getting too close to him, he was a good enough guy, and seeing him upset made me sad. Gah. "I think my guy might have some more information tomorrow. I'll let you know as soon as I do." Hopefully, Charles would have something to offer me that didn't point to Alfie. That watch thing was so bad. I'd noticed the glinting gold band when he was flipping Graham off. It surprised me that a farmer would have such a nice watch. I had no idea what brand it was, but maybe I should ask Charles to find out. If the guy had an expensive watch but little money, it would be suspect and give me further fuel to look into who else he was withholding money from yet claiming he didn't have any. If it was a cheap watch, well, I could ignore it, except to say that Alfie had it at home. And we were back to a depressing conclusion. That was a piece of evidence I did not want to impart to Finn. But then again, how long should I let him hope?

When I knew for sure.

I really needed to get to the farm again and see if I could speak to his ghost, provided he hadn't gone to the light or dark already. Hmm, maybe someone else could help me. I grabbed my phone off the table and stood. "Just going to the loo."

Finn gave a nod. It was telling that he didn't have a smarty-pants comment. Carina said, "Do you need company?"

"Ha ha, definitely not." At least no one had asked why I needed my phone. I had the urge to tell them that I wasn't taking toilet selfies, but maybe they weren't anywhere near thinking that.

She grinned. "Thanks be to the Gods. Why do women always have to go toged'er?"

I shrugged. "No idea. Don't miss me." I grinned, then walked towards the door that led to the back of the pub. As soon as I was through the door, I glanced back—Finn and Carina were chatting, and neither of them was watching. Instead of heading to the toilets—there was probably someone in there because tonight was busy—I headed outside to the car park. Meg's grandmother didn't go far from the pub, but she'd likely hear me from a few metres from the building.

I glanced around. Coast was clear, so I lifted my phone to my ear and said, "Mary, hello? Mary, it's Avery. I need to talk to you." *Please come.*

She materialised in front of me, smiling. "Hello, Avery, darling. How are you?"

I returned her smile. "I'm good thanks. How are you?"

"Oh, you know… still dead." She laughed.

Okay, so that was too funny, and I had to chuckle. "You're hilarious. I actually needed to ask you a question about two nights ago, although you probably won't know which night was which, so I guess just the situation."

Her expression turned serious. "Of course. What do you want to know?"

"Do you know who Mr Donigal the farmer is?"

She didn't even hesitate. "Oh, yes. He comes in here all the time. What about him?"

"The last time he was here, he was with a young man called Alfie. Do you know who he is?"

"Yes, I do. He's one of Bailey's acquaintances. He comes in sometimes." She cocked her head to the side. "Actually, I do remember them being here. Was that the night they had an argument? Bailey threw Alfie out. He's usually such a nice young man, and I was concerned about him."

I let out a relieved breath. "Yes, that's the night." Now, hopefully, she might have been curious as to what was going on.

"After Mr Donigal left, did you follow him out to the car park? I'm wondering if he and Alfie left in separate cars."

"I followed Alfie out." *Yes!* "Mr Donigal is an old man who can take care of himself. He's played the sympathy card a few times, and my grandchildren fall for it. He's had more than one free beer here over the years."

"And what happened?"

"Alfie got on his pushbike and rode away. He'd left by the

time Mr Donigal came out. I saw him get in his car. After that, I left."

Interesting. "Does Meg have security cameras out here?"

"Only the one." She pointed to the corner of the building. "But it mostly gets the area around the back door. Usually trouble starts there when people are stumbling out drunk. So they both would've been seen leaving but not what happens afterwards."

"Why don't they have cameras that take the whole car park?"

"Oh, they do, but it's voice activated. The patrons complained about their privacy—they're old school and were worried about Big Brother monitoring their every move." She chuckled. "We don't generally get trouble anyway. Manesbury isn't exactly a rowdy village, so Meg and Bailey decided not to push it. They came up with that compromise, so if someone was being attacked and screamed out, the camera would work, but if it's just normal comings and goings, it doesn't record."

"Oh, okay. I suppose it's the same with other businesses in the village, then? A couple of them must have cameras though. I was pretty sure in the last case, they'd gotten security video of a car passing through the main street."

"To be honest, I've never taken notice, but you're probably right. You'd have to check in with each business."

"Okay, thanks. You've been a huge help."

"My pleasure. It's been lovely chatting, Avery. I'll see you later." She waved, then disappeared. I lowered my phone. So, that was one clue against Alfie having done it. Now we just needed a few more.

# CHAPTER 8

The next morning, I was extra observant as I walked to work. From what I could see, the supermarket and post office were the two buildings that had security cameras. At least one of them should work, and they were at opposite ends of the village. They might not have filmed Alfie, since he could've ridden home via back streets, but they should've picked up Donigal as he drove. Note to self: find out where Alfie's friends lived. If they lived in a different direction to Donigal's farm, it would be confirmation that he went home first, and I trusted Charles when he told me that. If he then went out again and drove past the cameras, it could go some way to proving Alfie didn't do it, but by then, it would've been dark and hard to prove how many people and even who was in the car. But at this point, I'd take whatever evidence I could. Eventually, I'd go to Bellamy with what I knew, but I needed more if I didn't want him being annoyed and telling me to leave it alone. Also, when he asked how I knew what I knew, things could go south very quickly. MacPherson had to wear it when I said "my source," but could the police order me to tell them or possibly hold me as an accessory?

I would figure that out when it came to that.

I'd run out of coffee at home—major drama—so I stopped in at Heavenly Brew. One of my two arch nemeses was there. She gave me a quick frown as I lined up behind the customer she was serving—a tall, broad-shouldered man in his thirties whose tailored shorts, casual white shirt, and leather boat shoes looked out of place. He wore an expensive-looking watch and gold bracelet. "Thanks, Joy, gorgeous. I've missed your coffees." There was something about the way he said "coffees" that made me think coffee was a metaphor, and I did not need that image before I got mine.

She pushed her chest out. "I hear you're single again. Is that true?"

I couldn't see his face, but his voice sounded nonchalant. "Yeah. We called it quits a couple of weeks ago. Driving to London was becoming a bore."

"Well… if you want to… catch up any time, let me know." She tilted her head down a fraction and looked up at him with full-moon eyes, and I swear I vomited in my mouth just a bit. He'd better be careful because she was probably the human equivalent of a praying mantis—he wasn't going to survive a romp with her without severe repercussions. "I'm sorry about your dad, by the way. Any news?"

"No. But until they find a body, I won't believe he's not coming home alive. Thanks for asking." He turned, looked at me, then back at Joyless. "Sorry for holding you up." Oh, wow, this was the son. What did he do for a job because he definitely wasn't hiding his wealth? I doubted he worked for his father full-time. He wasn't what I expected.

She giggled. "Don't worry. Avery doesn't mind. Do you?"

"Not at all. My doctor's appointment isn't for another twenty minutes. I might have foot and mouth disease." I smiled.

He stepped to the side, away from me, and her face contorted into what could only be called a disgusted expression. Job done. "What do you want? I'll do it quickly."

"Just the usual. Skim milk cappuccino, thanks." I put the right money on the counter and leaned against it. She stepped back and stared at me.

"Step away from the counter. I don't want your gross disease."

"Oh, I'm sorry." I stepped away, and she gathered the money and put it in the register. I waited till she'd scratched her face to say, "Oh, you might want to wash your hands. It's super contagious."

If looks could kill, she'd be deadlier than a lightning strike. She ran to the sink, washed her hands, and scrubbed her face. When she was done, she came back and made my coffee. "I'm going to have to put on new make-up because of you. Don't come back here until you're over your disgusting disease." Coffee made, she hurriedly sprinkled chocolate powder on the top and shoved it towards me on the counter, stepping back as I moved forward to take it.

"Thanks. Have a great day!" I left, smiling. What a fun way to start the day. And I'd kind of met Donigal's son. Hopefully he'd never find out that Finn and I promised Tom that his family would pay their debt because he looked big enough to take Finn out. As fit as Finn was, he wasn't as big as that guy. Donigal's son had a longer reach, which counted for a lot when punches were thrown. I crossed my fingers that Tom would just send another letter rather than make a phone call. Things could get messy if he did that. There were bound to be security cameras in that shop. Hopefully they only held onto stuff for twenty-four hours. Could we be so lucky?

I turned into the laneway that held the MacPherson Media building. Well, this was unexpected. Charles stood a few feet from the building. He waved. I put my phone to my ear and smiled. "Hey, how's it going?"

"Good. I have some news about the case, but you're not going to like it."

My smile vanished. "Oh." I sighed. "Hit me with it."

"Mr Donigal had been underpaying Alfie for months, and Alfie sent him a letter a couple of weeks ago. Instead of paying him the wages, he fired him. Sergeant Bellamy said to another officer that the motive is even stronger now. He really thinks Alfie did it."

"Finn isn't going to like this. I'm going to have to say something. I was hoping I could keep things to myself, but he's going to find out eventually."

"But if you tell him, he'll think your informant is a police officer because who else would know? And then, won't you get a grilling from the sergeant?"

"Maybe. But he can't prove anything. It might make him reluctant to share things with his officers though, and what if he decided to blame one of them, and they got in trouble or lost their job because of me. Argh!" I had to the urge to grip my hair and pull. That saying existed for a reason. "Was there anything else?"

"No."

"Okay, well, thanks for letting me know. I'll check in with you this arvo. Okay?"

He gave a nod. "Yep. Bye, Avery."

As soon as he disappeared, another ghost appeared. I only knew she was a ghost because she popped into existence from nowhere. She wore jeans and a white tank top, was maybe thirty years old, and wore her wavy blonde hair in a ponytail. She smiled at me. "Hi, are you Avery the journalist?"

I kept my phone where it was. "Ah, yes. And you are?"

"My name's Cathy. I died a year ago today—heart attack."

"Oh, I'm sorry. That's so young to die of one."

"Yeah. I was competing in a marathon, and my heart just gave out. I thought I was fit and healthy, but apparently I had a congenital defect I knew nothing about."

"That sucks. I'm assuming I might be able to help you somehow?" Random ghosts didn't often pop up to say hello, which was something to be thankful for. They normally kept to themselves.

"Yes." She blushed as if embarrassed. "Sorry to be a bother, but my two-year wedding anniversary with my husband is coming up in a few days, and he's still really down. He's not dating. Other than going to work, he stays at home and drinks. I'm worried about him, and even though it's going to hurt, I want him to find someone else and be happy. I can't move on until I know that he's okay, and I'm ready. I hate this in-between. Seeing my loved ones and friends and not being able to talk to them or interact, well, it's frustrating and heart-breaking. I have a feeling that things will get better once I'm gone, and maybe me being here is holding Dan back as well. It might be a Catch-22 type of thing. But, anyway, this is my anniversary present to him."

Wow, that was sad and beautiful. "Setting him free is your present. That's touching and brave. I don't mean to interfere, but I'm going to ask you: Are you sure? I'd hate to set things in motion, and then you change your mind, and it's too late."

She smiled, and there was more determination in it than sadness. "Yes. I've been thinking about this for a while, and

I'm ready. I know he really wants kids, too, and I have a feeling if I don't let him go soon, he'll miss his chance. Time moves differently here, and I only know our anniversary is coming because he told someone about it and marks each day I've been gone on the calendar. Sometimes I turn up and he's marked the next day, but sometimes I think it's been a day, and it's been two weeks. I can't risk it anymore. He needs to live before it's too late."

"Okay. So, you'd like me to put a letter to the dead in the paper?"

Her smile widened. "Yes, please. I'd very much like that."

"Okay, consider it done. What's the date of your anniversary?" She told me, and I put it in my notes on my phone. "Can you tell me a few other things about your husband and marriage that others wouldn't necessarily know? He needs to believe what I put in there." As she spoke, I typed as quickly as I could. It would have been better to have a notepad, but this was what it was. It would look weird if I got all that out of my bag right now. After a few minutes, she finished. "I'll call out to you from here in a couple of days and read you what I've got. You can tell me if it's what you want, and I'll take it from there."

"Thank you so much, Avery. You're an angel. I'll see you soon." She waved, then disappeared.

What a busy morning. I looked at my phone. It was only nine fifteen, but it felt like lunchtime.

I headed straight up to the office. Today I was doing a follow-up article on Mr Donigal's disappearance. Even though Charles had given me some information, it was an excuse to call Bellamy and see if he would talk to me. I could beg for even a titbit of information. At this stage anything was better than nothing and might give us a new direction to go in.

Finn was the only one in. He looked up as I entered. "Did you have trouble sleeping?" I asked.

"Oh, you noticed my bags?"

Argh, how to let someone down gently? "Yeah. And I'm sorry to have to do this, but I have some bad news."

He didn't even sit up straighter or look eager. "If you're going to tell me that they found Mr Donigal's watch at Alfie's, I already know. I keep pestering Bellamy for information, and he finally caved. He said I needed to accept that he did it."

I blew out a breath and put my stuff on the table. "I'm sorry, Vinegar." Calling him by his proper name seemed weird. Maybe it would do him good to keep things as light as possible. "Did he tell you anything else?"

"No. He said they had other evidence that ties him to the disappearance, and they've laid charges. They're just waiting for the body to turn up."

"I assume they've interrogated Alfie about that?"

He shrugged. "I have no idea, but we'd have to assume."

"Right, so he's a fairly nice guy, not a hardened criminal. Surely he's still pleading his innocence and can't tell them where the body is. You'd think they'd take it as a clue that maybe he didn't do it and that they should keep looking." Hmm, I'd have to ask Charles about that. He'd done so well in finding out information, I had to hope he'd made sure he was there for every interview. "I wonder if he could ask to take a lie-detector test."

Hope had elbowed its way into his gaze again. "That might be a good idea. But I'd hate to ask about it if Alfie didn't want to do it. I really need to talk to him, but Bellamy won't let me."

I sat and got my laptop out. Finn looked so down that if I went over there, I'd probably give him a hug... and the wrong impression. I didn't know him well enough to say it was because I was his friend. Best just stay here. "I was thinking of calling him later, see if he had any information he could give me for my article. Maybe I can plead your case?"

"I'm sure it couldn't hurt. A couple of weeks ago, I would've said you'll make my life harder, but he's had a few positive things to say about you since you helped with that last case. He's sworn me to secrecy, so I can't elaborate." One corner of his mouth curled up. He loved messing with me.

I grinned. "That's okay. I can imagine he said some wonderful things because I *am* awesome."

From across the room, his gaze bored into mine. "You totally are."

He was probably joking, but my cheeks heated. *Don't take him seriously. He's a player.*

He cleared his throat. "Are you ready for tonight?"

Tonight? Oh, right. "No. What about you?"

"I wish I hadn't said yes."

I rolled my eyes. "Your desire to see me suffer was such that you dropped yourself into it, so I have no sympathy. You've ruined both our evenings. It would serve you right if I didn't turn up."

He gave me a "yeah right" face. "Well, maybe *I* won't turn up. Besides, you'd be letting Meg down. As much as I love to give you a hard time, I know you're a good person. You wouldn't do that to a friend."

I narrowed my eyes. How dare he get it right. "Well, fine. But you better be there, because if I have to suffer, so do you, and if you're not there, I'll figure out how to make things horrible for you. Maybe I'll tell Joyless that you like her." Hmm, maybe he did like her. That probably wasn't a threat at all.

"Joyless?" He started laughing and was soon bent over in hysterics. When he had a handle on himself, he sat up. "You're hilarious. She's annoying, but she's not that bad. She's always nice to me."

"Yeah, I bet she is. I've found her more… challenging." I wasn't going to get into it with him, and I'd already let too much slip. He knew what my name for her was. Oops.

"Carina will probably agree with you, though. Those two have never gotten on."

"That's because Carina has impeccable taste." I unlocked my phone. "I'll call Bellamy now. Wish me luck."

"Ha, good luck. You're going to need it." *Yeah, thanks for the reminder.*

Would he even take my call?

"Cramptonbury Police Station. How can I help you?"

At least one thing had gone my way. "Hello, PC Adams. How's it going?"

"Oh, Avery. Hello! I'm good thanks. How are you?"

"I'm good, but I would be even better if I could speak to the sergeant. Is he in?" *Please put me through.*

I could hear the smile in her voice. "He's just having his morning cuppa. He was lamenting a lack of apple tart the other day. Just in case you're interested."

I chuckled. "Duly noted. I was thinking of baking this weekend, actually."

"I look forward to the results. Now, I'll just put you through."

My mouth dropped open. She wasn't even going to check. Ha! The gatekeeper was definitely on my side. Now I just better keep those tarts coming.

"Hello, Winters." He didn't ask what I wanted, which meant he didn't really want to know, but that was his bad luck.

A lack of enthusiasm wasn't going to stop me, which he also probably knew if his defeated tone of voice was anything to go by.

"Hello, Sergeant. There are a couple of things I wanted to discuss. The first is that I'm going to stop by on the weekend with another tart. I was going to do some baking, and the first person I thought of was you."

"Thank you. I will admit that I've been wondering when you might drop another one by."

"My pleasure. The second thing I wanted to ask was whether there was anything you could go on the record with in the Donigal case? I'm writing an update on Mr Donigal going missing, and I'm sure the good citizens of our village are wondering how things are travelling, so you're really talking to them. I realise you can't tell me everything, but just one small thing would be awesome. Do you think you're closer to finding Mr Donigal?" I would've said body because we both could probably guess that's where it was heading, but I didn't want to be negative.

"I'll tell you what I can. I will stand by my promise to help you when I'm able—you've helped me, and I never forget who I owe. You probably already know that we've charged Alfie Thomas. We found Mr Donigal's car outside a friends' of his. Forensics is still going over the car, so I have nothing to say about that. At this stage, it's looking like a murder investigation, but we haven't found the body. It might be some time, but we have reason to believe we'll find it within ten miles of the village. We'll let the public know as soon as we have something."

"Thank you so much!" Okay, so I wasn't super excited to be told what I already knew, but it was nice that he was cooperating without me having to beg. Now for the last question—

unfortunately I wasn't going to tell him about Graham Field because I promised, and I didn't need that guy hating me. Who knew what he was capable of? If I got some solid evidence, I'd take it to Bellamy, but until then, Finn and I would keep it to ourselves. "I have one more thing to ask. I hope I'm not overstepping any boundaries, but, to be honest, Vinegar is being a pain in the butt." He knew my name for Finn was Vinegar, and I was hoping the nickname would make this conversation more personal. Finnegan looked at me, his forehead scrunched. I smirked. "He's worried about Alfie and really needs to talk to him. Alfie hasn't exactly had an easy time of it, and Vinegar is adamant that he needs the support. I guess he doesn't want him to do anything foolish, like suicide. Plus, of course, he wants to be there for his friend. There's a chance he didn't do it... at least that's what Vinegar thinks. And to be honest, someone could've planted the watch and the car to incriminate him."

There was a long pause. Finn was staring at me, obviously hoping for the best. I shrugged. Just as I was going to ask if he was still there, he said, "It's against protocol, but I'll give him five minutes supervised access. He can come down in thirty minutes. But neither of you are allowed to report on what was said. Understood?"

"Yes, sir. I promise whatever's said in that meeting won't go further than Vinegar or me." Finnegan raised his brows as if to say "I didn't promise to tell you anything." I raised a brow and muted the phone. "You owe me for this, so that's what you have to do." I unmuted it while he pulled a face.

"Okay, send him down here, then. And I expect that tart on my desk by Monday."

"Yes, sir. Bye." I grinned. He was fairly easy to please. If I could keep him in tarts, he would hopefully keep me in the loop. I hung up and looked at Finn. "You can have five minutes with him in half an hour, so I'd get your butt down there soon if I were you. You heard the deal on that though."

He smiled. "I did—I hate people making promises on my behalf, but you did good, kid. Thanks."

"My pleasure. And you're going to tell me everything."

He stared at me, possibly trying to come up with an argument against it, but the tension left his shoulders, and he nodded. "Fine. I guess I do owe you that much."

"Thanks. Are you coming straight back here afterwards?"

"No. I have an appointment after that. I'll probably be in at lunchtime. I'll update you then. I'm pretty sure he's just going to say he's innocent. Anyway, I'm off." He stood, packed up his stuff, and left while I got to work on my updated article.

Ah, poop. I just remembered I forgot to ask Bellamy something. I stared at my phone. Should I, or shouldn't I? Hmm, maybe not right now. I'd see if Charles could help me first. I grabbed my phone as a cover. "Charles, hello? I need to talk to you."

He appeared in front of my desk. "Hi. What is it?"

"I was hoping you could go to Donigal's farm and look at what cars are there. I need the make and model of each one, plus the number plates. Can you do that?"

He cocked his head to the side. "Yeah, I s'pose so. Do I have to do it now?"

"Sometime today would be great, but since you can't tell time very well, maybe do it now and come straight back. Sorry to be a pain."

Erin materialised and looked up at Charles, who was a few inches taller than her. She smiled shyly. "Hello, Charles. How are you?"

He smiled. "I'm good thanks. How are you?"

"Oh, you know. A bit bored."

"Do you want to come to a farm with me?"

Her eyes lit up. "Yes, please! Are there horses?"

He nodded. "You bet." He started glowing, and it spread over her.

"Ooh, what's that light?" I asked.

"It's a link to me so she doesn't get lost."

Erin looked at me. "I can't feel it, but I can see it, and it guides me through the travel corridors."

I blinked. "Travel corridors?" This was the first I'd heard about that.

"We have corridors and portals. How else do you think we get everywhere so quickly?" Charles looked at me as if I were stupid.

"Well, excuse me if I'm not up to date with how spirits get around. Silly me."

He rolled his eyes, then looked at Erin. "Ready?"

"You bet."

They disappeared, and I smiled at how sweet it was that two of my ghost friends were getting to know each other. The world was truly weirder than I ever gave it credit for.

❧

MacPherson had a job for me at a town about thirty minutes' drive away. It was a local TV star who'd won some viewers' favourite award, and I had to wait around to ask my questions. The actor was giving everyone five minutes. Oh joy. By the time I did all that and got back, Finn was gone again, so I didn't get to talk to him. So I had to wait till I saw him at the pub, and even then we only had five minutes during the event to talk—when it was our turn to speed "date." Other than that, I'd have to talk to him afterwards, and it didn't finish till nine.

As I stood in the doorway and observed everyone in the pub, guilt nibbled at my conscience. I turned up only because I'd promised Meg, but I didn't want to encourage any of the men, so I'd worn jeans and a T-shirt and no make-up—zero effort, except the walking-here bit. My hair was in a messy bun because it was warm, and I hated having a hot, sweaty neck.

I'd also brought my notepad and pen for the breaks, so I could record how my dates had gone before I forgot the little details. I wasn't sure what angle my story was going to have yet, but I was positive it would reveal itself to me by the time the night was over.

The room was full of young people. Some of them were what I'd call attractive, and others not so much. At least to my taste. The women's fashion choices leaned towards lots of cleavage, sky-high heels, and fake caterpillar eyelashes. I had no doubt I could look so much more attractive with that kind of help, but the carrot wasn't big enough for me tonight to bother. Hmm, I was *so* excited to be here. The sarcasm was strong in me tonight. Maybe I should check my attitude before I made everyone else sad. I plastered a smile on and stepped into the room.

I headed straight for the bar. Meg's dad was serving, along with another guy I'd never seen before who looked to be in his thirties, with sandy-brown curly hair and a friendly smile. The new guy didn't waste any time when I reached the bar. "What can I get you?" He had an American accent.

"A house white, thanks."

He turned to get a glass, and Meg's dad gave me a nod. "Hello, Avery. Giving the sergeant hell lately?"

I chuckled. "Just a little bit. Have to keep him on his toes."

Meg's dad laughed and went to serve someone at the other end of the bar. The new guy put my drink on the counter and asked for the money. I gave it to him. "Are you going to be working here on the regular?"

"I am." He put his hand out to shake mine. "Mike."

I shook his hand. "Avery. Nice to meet you."

"Likewise. You here for the dating thing?"

"Under duress from Miss Meg, yes." I grinned. "The things we do for our friends."

He returned my grin. "Indeed. Well, enjoy the night."

"Thanks." Right, so this must mean that Bailey'd been roped in as well. Great. I had to sit opposite two of the hottest guys in the village, and probably the county, and pretend I wasn't all hot and bothered. Okay, so it was a first-world problem, but still. Oh, and it was only for five minutes. What was I, an amateur? Hmm, kind of. Brad was the only guy I'd been in a proper relationship with. Before him, I'd gone on a couple of dates with other guys, but my experience wasn't what I'd call substantial. Maybe tonight would be good for me to see what other men were like, at least how entertaining they could be in five minutes. And who knew? Maybe I'd hit it off with a couple of them in a platonic way and widen my circle of friends. It wasn't like anything bad could come of this. Other than me being not that into it, I was going to get an article out of the event, some dating experience, and a good cause would get some money. Surprise, surprise, this appeared to be a win-win-win. Who knew?

So, it was just how you looked at it.

I found Meg. She was talking to Finn and the young guy from the butchers—Luke. If he were a cartoon character, there'd be hearts shooting from his eyes while he stared at

Meg. I chuckled. She had that long-distance thing going on, but maybe she should look closer to home. "Hey." I smiled.

Meg threw her arms around me, and a dribble of wine jumped out onto my arm. "Avery, you made it!"

I gave her a "look." "I told you I was coming. I'm a woman of my word. I'm nothing if not reliable."

Finn grinned. "Lead with that on your dates. The guys will love it. Maybe one will offer you a job?" He was such a smart bum. Luke chuckled. Typical male idiot sense of humour. So not funny.

"I'll make sure to use it on the guys I'm not attracted to." I smiled sweetly, knowing that's what I'd lead with for our "date."

Bailey joined our group. His mouth dropped open at me, and he slapped his palms on his cheeks in mock surprise. "You came!"

I rolled my eyes and bit back a smile. It was pretty funny. "Yes, I did. I would never let Meg down. Besides, I'm going to write about it for the paper."

Bailey chuckled. "I'm just teasing you, but, um, are you writing about it to promote the event or to critique the male dating skills?"

I smirked. "A bit of both. I'd say be on your best behaviour, but that still wouldn't help Vinegar." Everyone laughed… except Finn, who pulled an unimpressed face.

Bailey patted Finn on the back. "He's a bit of a champion in the dating arena. I reckon that he's gone on more dates in the last two years than all of the guys in this room combined."

Luke grinned. "He's the man!"

Meg and I looked at each other and shook our heads. Again, typical boys.

Finn actually looked sheepish, which was weird, but he put

on a smirk. "Well, what can I say? The ladies love me? It's not my fault I was born this good-looking."

I laughed along with everyone else, but there was an undercurrent, like maybe he didn't want this attention, and maybe he was sick of being the village Lothario. But then again, if he didn't want that title, he could always date less or decide to date one person for a while. Anyway, it wasn't my problem.

Meg looked around the group. "Everyone got a drink? Let's get organised. We're going to ring the bell in a few minutes. I have to give a speech and hand out the free-drink voucher. I'll be back." She grabbed the vouchers from behind the bar and returned, handing us one each, except Bailey since I was sure he could put his mouth under the beer tap and turn it on, drink as much as he wanted, and not get in trouble because he was part-owner of the establishment. Meg gave one to everyone else, and then she stood on a box next to the bar and rang the small bell that sat atop the black granite top.

She smiled and waved at everyone as the chatter petered off to silence. "Thanks, everyone, for coming and supporting our dating night. All proceeds will go to preventing youth suicide." She paused as everyone clapped, led by Bailey. "Everyone should have their voucher for one free alcoholic beverage. It includes house wine, beer, and cider."

Some clown yelled out, "No top-shelf stuff then?"

She chuckled. "No, Justin, and if you ask me a third time, I'm going to take away the voucher you have." Everyone laughed. She held her hand up to encourage silence again. "We have an exceptional turnout tonight, so thank you. We have thirty-five minutes of dating and half an hour break for nibbles. Then we'll get back to our last thirty-five minutes of dating. You'll get five minutes with each person, and a minute between 'dates,' so make your changeovers quick. You'll have time at the end of the night to exchange numbers if you want, so don't muck around with that once the bell's rung. You'll each get twelve dates, which means you won't get to meet everyone here, but if someone catches your eye, I'm sure you can have a chat in the break or afterwards. Any questions?"

Oh, God, twelve dates sounded like a lot. Hopefully, they wouldn't all be boring or awkward. What were the odds? Hmm, I could've asked the same question of getting hit by lightning….

Meg continued, "You'll see we've set the tables up as two-seaters. Each table has a number on it. It's the guys who are going to move. Wherever you start, go to the next consecutive number. When you get to table thirty, you then go to table one. Does everyone understand?" There were a lot of affirmative noises. "Great. Ladies, if you'll each sit at a table. Once you're all settled, I'll ring the bell, and I'd like the gentlemen to go to the table number that's on the back of your drink voucher." Wow, she'd thought of everything. Impressive. Although, I noted that she wasn't going to a table. The hide! She'd told me she was doing it too. Grrr. I felt so duped.

The women moved to their tables, some of them running, as if we were playing musical chairs. *Chill, ladies. There're no points for sitting down first.* Two women got into an argument over one table. I shared a look with Meg. She bit her lip to keep from laughing, but I wasn't hosting, and I could do what I wanted. There were two tables left, and I chose the one next to the window. It felt more protected, like maybe no one would notice me, and I could get away with eavesdropping on the other dates without having to do one myself.

Life was not that kind.

I put my bag at my feet and took out my notepad and pen

—just in case things got really interesting and I couldn't keep up. Would it look weird? Definitely. Did I care? Nope. Would it ensure no one would be asking for my number later? Most probably. I smiled. It was good to have a plan.

By the time Meg rang the bell, my palms were sweating. Gross.

Two guys speed-walked to my table. Seriously? What's wrong with you, dudes? Compared to the other ladies here, I was a plain-Jane. Maybe they wanted to get the worst over and done with first. I chuckled. Okay, so I was being hard on myself, but it was fun sometimes. They neared the table, and the taller, beefier one managed to shoulder check the other guy out of the way and slide into the seat opposite me. He grinned as if nothing terribly childish had just happened and held out his hand across the table. "Hi, I'm Oscar."

"Hi, Oscar. I'm Avery." I briefly considered not wiping my sweaty palm on my jeans, but I didn't want to be known as the slimy Aussie, so I did, then shook his hand. "Lovely to meet you."

"Likewise." Oscar was about five foot eleven and had fair, thinning hair. But I was going to ignore that because I wasn't here to find a husband. Besides, I knew that when I was ready to date legitimately, if a guy had a personality I adored, whether he had hair or not wouldn't bother me. The only issue was getting past that to get to know someone. I wasn't a shallow person—at least I didn't think so—but the butterflies liked what they liked. It wasn't my fault. "So, Avery, where are you from. You have an accent, but I can't quite place it."

"Australia." I would've thought it was distinctive, but what did I know?

He chuckled. "Ah, good. I was thinking it might be New Zealand, the place with the sheep."

I laughed. "Ah, no. But we're close."

"You are. So, if you're from Australia, do you know Patty Thomas? She lives in Perth. She's my aunt on my mother's side."

I blinked. Was this guy joking? The way he was staring at me, waiting for my answer, made me think not. "I've never been to Perth. I'm from Sydney."

"Oh, are they not close together?"

I shrugged. "Depends if you call roughly 4000 kilometres far or not. Up to you. I hate to be the one to break it to you, but there are about twenty-eight million people in Australia. I don't know everyone."

He blushed. "Oh, yeah, right. Sorry."

Gah, now I felt bad. "Don't worry about it. Happens all the time." I smiled kindly.

He smiled too. "Phew! So I'm not an idiot?"

*Depends on your definition of an idiot.* "Not at all. So, what do you do for work?"

"Why do women always ask that? It's like they're waiting to judge you."

"Um, I'm just making small talk. Don't answer if you don't want. I know… what's your favourite colour?" Could this get any worse? *No, Avery. Don't ask.* I tapped the tabletop since it was wood.

"Black. Some people say it's not a colour, but it is. You can see it, right? It's the darkest of all the colours. People have no idea."

"No, they don't. How they get by in the world, well, I have no idea." *Maybe you could explain it to me?*

Meg rang the bell. Thanks be to the dating gods.

He stood. "It was nice meeting you. Maybe I could get your number later."

I smiled. "I'll think about it. I only wanted to give my number to one person tonight, so I'll make my decision when I've done all the dates."

"Oh, cool. Great idea. I just planned to get everyone's numbers. You know, improve my odds of landing someone."

The next guy was standing there, waiting to sit. "Time's up, buddy. Don't keep the next lady waiting." My saviour, or was it my next torturer, managed to move him along, and he sat. He was about six foot tall and slender. His moustache looked like the end of a broom... one of the witchy ones. It wasn't a good look. In other news, he had all his hair. It was dark and wavy and quite acceptable. "I'm Timothy, and you are?"

"Avery."

"Do you wear glasses at all?"

I wasn't sure where he was going with this, but we only had five minutes to fill. Might as well go along with it. "I wear sunglasses sometimes." *Like any other normal person.*

"No, like librarian's glasses. I have a thing for women who wear glasses." He pulled a pair of sparkly purple-framed reading glasses from his shirt pocket. "Here, try these on." Now the creepy moustache made sense. The look in his eyes was... disconcerting.

My filter had no time to engage, and I barked out a laugh. He stared at me as if I were an undone Rubik's Cube™ that he was supposed to solve. "Ah, no. You do know that's a weird request."

He put the glasses back in his pocket. "I'm trying to save us time. There's no point going any further if you're not into wearing glasses."

"I'm sorry that my vision is fine. Maybe I'll call you when I'm forty. I think that's about the time eyesight declines. I'll probably be right into glasses when that happens."

He leaned back and folded his arms. "I'll probably be married with kids by then. It'll be too late."

"Oh. What. A. Shame."

*Tinkle, tinkle.* Gah, next!

"Goodbye, Avery."

"Bye, Timothy." *May we never cross paths again.* I was totally going to kill Meg when this was over.

Meg's grandmother appeared next to me, laughing. "Oh, my. The quality of men has really deteriorated since Arthur and I were courting. Good luck, Avery." She disappeared, just like I wanted to.

"Take me with you," I whispered.

"Pardon me?" A muscly guy with a shaved head sat opposite me. He wore a blue short-sleeved shirt and tan cargo-style pants. Tattoos covered both arms and peeked out of his shirt to halfway up his neck. I wasn't against tattoos, but this was next level, and they weren't my thing. It was becoming apparent that I was very picky. Meh, I could adjust my standards when I decided to start dating for real.

"Oh, sorry, just talking to myself. The last guy was… not my type." I smiled. "I'm Avery. What's your name?"

Okay, other than his overall bikie vibe, he had large muscles—obviously worked out, which wasn't a bad thing—and his face was cute. Blue eyes, clean-shaven, and good bone structure. His looks were promising, but what was going to happen when he opened his mouth and let his personality come out?

"I'm Carl. I'm a landscape gardener, and I love to read. Tell me about yourself." He smiled. Well, this was refreshing—a normal person.

"I'm a journalist, and I only recently moved here from Sydney, Australia. I love to read as well. What kind of books are you into?"

"Thrillers, biographies, and occasionally sci-fi. What about you?"

"Mysteries, thrillers, romance. I even enjoy a bit of literary fiction every now and then. I really appreciate the art of literary fiction, the way some writers can structure a sentence to be the most beautiful and profound thing ever. But mostly, I just want to escape, and mystery and romance are perfect for that." If he was going to judge me for reading romances, he was getting a big fat cross next to his name.

"Are you enjoying it here so far?" Imagine that—he didn't make fun of me. Nice.

We chatted for the rest of the short time, and I was actually a bit disappointed when the bell rang. He got up and said goodbye, ushering in my next torturer. Ryan was twenty-two and a half. Seriously, who says and a half? Normally six-year-olds. "And how old are you, Avery?"

"Twenty-six."

His eyes widened. "Oh, that's old. I never date women older than me."

"Well, I'm in luck, then." It was time to open the notebook. I wrote quickly and made some points about each date.

"What are you doing?"

I looked up at him. "I don't want to forget the highlights of each date, so I'm making some notes." That should eat up a minute or two. Hmm, maybe I should get some more intel. "Why don't you like dating older women, Ryan?"

He leaned back in his chair and puffed his chest out. "They're bossy, and some of the stuff they like to talk about is bo-ring. And they want kids. They're just out to settle down and stop me from having fun."

I nodded. "Mmm, you make a good point. I think you're doing them a favour by not dating them. They want someone they can rely on, which is obviously not you." I smiled, and so did he, but his eyes were lit with confusion. He wasn't sure if I was agreeing with him for the right reasons. He would be correct in his suspicions, but the bell dinged, and he was out of thinking time. Poor Ryan. I gave a wave as he stood. "See ya." I sighed. One out of four dates being okay was dismal, or was that normal? I peered around the room. Hmm, I'd have to interview some of these women and get their take on the odds. They were probably all consistently dating and had more experience than just this event.

The next guy's name was Raven, and that was the most exciting thing about him. He wasn't stupid or unattractive or ridiculous, but he was shy and only managed about three sentences. He basically blushed the whole time and looked at the table. At least he was trying. I was pretty sure we were both relieved when the five minutes was up. Woohoo, only one date to go before half-time. I could barely stand it, but it was almost done. My shoulders slumped. Oh, yeah, half-time. Could I live through another session of this?

"Hi, I'm Paul." A lanky, attractive guy with chocolate-brown eyes stuck his hand towards me as he sat. "Nice to meet you." Okay, good start. I was interested to see how he would disappoint me. And, yes, maybe my attitude had slipped into the negative, but, honestly, could you blame me? Also, I was giving the guy a chance to pleasantly surprise me. It wouldn't take much at this point. The other guys had done him a favour.

"Hi, Paul. I'm Avery. Nice to meet you too. What do you

do for work?" Yes, I was leading with this question. Might as well get any potential triggers out of the way.

"I'm an accountant. I work in Exeter. What do you do?" Ooh, okay, so we'd reached the thirty-second mark with no disasters.

"I'm a journalist. I work for the *Manesbury Daily.*"

He narrowed his eyes. "You're a journalist?"

I was fairly sure that's what I'd just said. "Um, yeah. Is that a problem?"

He shrugged. "Not really. You just don't look like one."

"What is one supposed to look like?"

He considered for a moment. "Well, a man, for a start. They have those newsreader ladies on the TV, but they're there just for looks. The male reporters do all the real work, and they write all the hard-hitting stories."

I rubbed my forehead. This was beyond painful. "It's really weird, you know?"

"What's weird?"

"That you look so normal, but you've actually time-travelled from the fifties. How did you do that?"

*Ringringringringring.*

And that was my cue to get the hell out of this chair. I grabbed my notebook and bag, stood, and stomped to Meg. She was totally going to cop it. Her eyes widened when she saw my face. "Yikes, Avery. What's wrong?"

I whisper hissed. "Did you troll the area for the biggest idiots or what? I've had one nice guy out of six. They make my ex look good. And how come you're not participating? I thought you were."

She gave me a cheesy grin. "Someone has to ring the bell. Besides, I have a boyfriend."

I blew out a big breath. "Fine!" She was in a long-distance

relationship, so I couldn't very well argue. They'd seen each other once since Chris moved to Scotland, and he hadn't been gone that long, so maybe they would make it work?

"Looking on the bright side, you must have plenty of material for an article."

I laughed. "There is that, I suppose. Okay, I'll stop complaining, but maybe I need three more wines to get me through the rest of it."

Finn had snuck up behind me. "You have to work tomorrow, don't forget, miss wino."

I turned. "Yes, I know, but I also have to sit through six more dates, and if I don't get through that with my sanity intact, I'll need a day off tomorrow."

"Well, I thought we could talk shop on the walk home, and it would be great if you could think logically and talk to me without slurring." He raised a brow.

"Oh, right. I forgot. Sorry." Jeeze, these dates had really thrown me. How could I forget about finding out what Alfie said?

He put his hand on his heart. "Oh, how you wound me."

A gorgeous blonde woman who looked like a model with her long legs and five-foot ten height (okay, so two inches of that was probably her stilettos) came up to us. She smiled at Finn.

I gave him a "you have to be kidding" look. "I very much doubt that."

"Hi, Finny. Thanks for the date. You're the best so far." Meg and I shared a look at the woman's gushing critique. "Here's my number." She handed him her card.

He took it and unleashed his butterfly-conjuring smile. "Thanks." Interestingly, he didn't give her his number. "I'll call you sometime."

Her smile faded. Yikes. We'd all heard that line before. I actually felt bad for her. She was putting herself out there, and bam! Shot down. I smiled at her. "Don't worry about him. He's actually shy, despite how he comes across. I'm sure he'll come to his senses when he's not in front of me and Meg. We tease him a lot."

"Oh, right." She gave me a grateful smile. "Thank you...?"

"Avery. Lovely to meet you. What's your name?"

"Stella."

"I wouldn't have thought you'd need to come to one of these. You must have the guys chasing you down the street." Or maybe they were too intimidated by her looks? I'd heard that super gorgeous women sometimes had a hard time because guys assumed they'd get shot down, so they didn't bother approaching them.

She chuckled. "Ah, no. I was dating someone, but he broke up with me two weeks ago."

Meg leaned in and touched her arm. "Oh, I'm so sorry. That's terrible." Then realisation lit in Meg's eyes. "Oh, I'm sorry. You were dating Danny, weren't you?"

Her face dropped into sadness. "Yes. I tried calling him to say sorry about his dad going missing, but he's blocked my number. I didn't even do anything to him. I just don't understand it."

Oh, wow, *that* Danny. "Well, it's his loss, clearly."

She gave me a sad smile. "Thanks, Avery. That's very kind of you."

"Can I ask what is going to seem like a weird question?"

She gave me a curious look. "Ah, yeah, sure."

"Did he get along with his dad?"

She nodded. "Very much so. He was an only child. I mean,

the farm is everything to his dad, but he understood when Danny didn't want to work on it anymore. He spends his time looking after his mum and DJing at night. It works for all of them. He's a good son. I got along well with Mr Donigal as well. I'm holding out hope that he'll be found alive."

"Okay, thanks, and us too. Mrs Donigal seemed really nice when I spoke to her." Okay, so she didn't really—not that she wasn't nice. She was in shock, and I doubt I saw much of who she really was.

"Why do you ask?"

"I'm covering the incident for the paper. Things are constantly changing, but it's good to have info to kind of sprinkle in there about their lives." I shrugged and glanced at Finn, who gave an almost imperceptible nod. The bigger the picture we could paint about Mr Donigal's life for ourselves, the better. Maybe Danny could vouch for Alfie? It was a long-shot because if the police thought Alfie killed his father, he probably wasn't going to hold any warm and fuzzies for him. But did he think he did it? It would be interesting to find out.

Bailey must've been on duty for half-time because he appeared next to me, holding a tray of smoked salmon, cream cheese, and dill blintzes. "Food, anyone?"

"Ooh, yum." Finger food was my favourite… well one of my favourites. I couldn't say no. "Can I have two?"

Bailey laughed. "Of course. A couple of the ladies have already turned them down, so there's more than enough. We have other stuff coming out too."

I grabbed my blintzes and popped one in my mouth. "Mmmmmmm. So good." Okay, so tonight could've been worse. I was getting delicious finger food and a story out of it, plus a small piece of information to add to the Donigal puzzle. Actually. "Stella?"

"Yes."

"Did the Donigals ever mention any trouble they had with the neighbour, Mr Field?"

She pressed her lips together, thinking. "Um, I remember going over there once with Danny after he'd stayed at my place, a couple of months ago, and Mr Field had just come out of the house. The door had slammed, and he looked angry. I asked Danny what it was about, and he said he didn't know. Said the guy had always been difficult and cranky, so I thought nothing of it. Come to think of it, Mr Donigal looked angry when I went inside, and Mrs Donigal had red eyes, as if she'd been crying. Neither of them said anything, and Danny didn't ask, so I pretended nothing was going on too."

"Okay, thanks. It could've just been a dispute over fences for all we know." I tried to play it down because maybe that's all it was, but why would Mrs Donigal have been crying? It didn't make sense.

She shrugged. "Who knows."

A guy—who wasn't half bad-looking—I hadn't met stood next to our group. "Stella, there you are. I've been wanting to talk to you."

She scrunched her eyes shut as if she didn't want to talk to him, then turned to face him. "Hi, Cory." Ha, maybe he'd been an annoying date. No wonder she was wanting to give her number to Finn. If her dates had been half as bad as mine, Finn and Bailey were definitely the two best catches within a ten-mile radius.

Bailey had wandered off with his tray, and Meg was chatting to Finn, so I slipped off to the ladies'. The noise in the pub made it hard to think, and the overload of personalities at my table had me needing a breather. I went to the loo, and when I was done, I closed the lid and sat on it for a minute.

Why would Mrs Donigal have been crying? Had one man threatened to kill the other? Were they fighting over her? Surely old people didn't bother getting that worked up. Hormones faded over time; you would think they didn't have it in them, but you never knew.

Gah, we needed more information. I really wanted to talk to Bellamy. There must be other suspects we were missing. I hadn't had to try very hard, and I found three people Mr Donigal was at odds with. There must be more, but Bellamy was hanging his hat on only one of them, not even looking for others. Did I want to go back on my word and dob Graham Field in? He'd answered our questions, and if there was no proof he'd done anything, Bellamy was just going to let him go, and then I'd have a new enemy. No thanks.

Where did that leave us? Maybe doing more research on why Field had changed his name. He had a secret, but was that secret pertinent to this situation? There was only one way to decide. And who was that guy supporting Mrs Donigal?

I shut my eyes and relaxed for a moment. *You can do this, Avery. Time to drag yourself back into the fray.*

I washed my hands and made my way back out. The chatter was louder than before, maybe increasing to match the level of alcohol consumption. Maybe my next batch of dates would be more enjoyable with a couple more wines under my belt. But then again, I had to work tomorrow, and I had a nine o'clock appointment, so no sleeping in. I sighed. Meg totally owed me.

Bailey came up to me with his tray of temptation. "Ooh, mini quiches. Don't mind if I do." I took three.

He chuckled. "You're easy to please."

"Hmm, maybe when it's food." I gazed around the room, then looked at Bailey. "Dating, not so much."

"Haven't had much luck tonight?"

"Not that I wanted to have any luck, but some of these guys are the worst examples of humans. One guy has a reading-glasses fetish." I shuddered. "Argh, talking about them is ruining my appetite."

"Quick, eat another quiche!" Bailey shoved one in my mouth, and I started laughing.

"Oh, mmmy, ggd." It was hard to laugh, eat, and talk at the same time, but I was doing my best.

The bell rang. Noooooooooo! I looked over at Meg, who stood on her box again, and she grinned at me. I ran my finger across my throat, then pointed at her. She just laughed. Grrr.

"Ha, see you in the bear pit, Avery."

I swallowed the food. "Yeah, good luck. I hope your night is better than mine."

"A couple of the ladies have been… hard work, but a few were really nice. I might get a phone number or two later." The way he stared at me… was he waiting for me to say something?

I smiled. "Well, they'd be lucky to get your number. Good luck!" Before he could read anything into that, I hurried to my torture chamber and got my notebook out again.

The next man to introduce himself was about my height and had a blond man bun. It wasn't really my thing, but he was nice enough. He introduced himself as he sat. "I'm Ed. How's it going?"

"Hi, Ed. I'm Avery, and I'm good, thanks. How are you?"

"Great. I love your accent. Australian I'm guessing?"

"Thanks, and yes. So, what brings you to a speed-dating night."

The conversation continued in a relaxed and *normal* way. Colour me surprised. When we said goodbye, my smile was genuine. He seemed like a good guy. The second man to sit opposite me was also normal person. Maybe I'd gotten all the weirdos out of the way in session one?

Date three proved me wrong. You know when you make toast, and you butter it, then put Vegemite on, and you're ready to eat it, and it falls on the floor, butter-side down—the disappointment is enough to make you want to cry. That was me when Xavier opened his mouth and spoke. "Have you seen some of those other chicks? One of them, Stella, oh, man, was she hot. Legs for days and those melons." He brought his fingers to his lips and kissed them like an Italian saying that his food was *bellissimo*. He stared at my chest, but there was nothing much to see since I was wearing a shapeless T-shirt. "You don't like to get the girls out?"

"Only on Sundays. I'm all about the mystery." I wondered if he understood sarcasm.

"Oh, it's a shame it's Thursday, then." That answered that question. He leaned forward and lowered his voice. "Would you be into sending me a nude?"

I slowly moved back to keep the distance between us comparable to what it was before he leaned in. "Do women usually say yes when you ask them?"

He looked at the table as if considering. "Well… not many, but enough do that I might as well ask." He brought out the creepy grin. "I'll send you a pic too."

"Mmm, I don't think so. I only send nudes to hot guys."

His eyes widened, and his mouth dropped open. He wanted to say something, but he hadn't worked it out yet. Finally, he did. "You're not exactly hot, you know. Your boobs are too small, and you give off a cold vibe, like a frigid fish."

I sucked my cheeks in and made a fish face, opening and closing my weirdly shaped lips. He stood quickly, his chair flying back. He didn't bother pushing it back in before taking three stompy steps. His exit wanted so much to be dramatic, but the next table was right there, and he stopped short. He folded his arms and turned his back to me while he waited at the next table for the bell to ring. He he he. I couldn't help laughing. I'd already asked this question tonight, but it begged repeating. Where did Meg find these idiots? I couldn't believe that out of the whole population, at least 50 per cent of men had substandard intelligence or emotional intelligence as tonight implied. If it was true, I'd be so depressed. It might explain how I ended up with Brad. Seemed the odds were never on my side.

Staying single gave me a much better chance of happiness. I smiled, secure in the decision I'd made before coming here. Solo was the way to go.

The bell rang. The guy getting up from the next table to come here had shaggy brown hair and a lithe build. He wore a black ACDC T-shirt and ripped jeans. A couple of tatts coloured one arm. He grabbed the chair and sat. His smile was friendly. "Hey, I'm Mark."

"Hey, Mark. I'm Avery. How are you?"

"I'm good thanks. Great night, hey?"

If I told him my truth, he'd have to listen to whingeing for the whole five minutes, so I did what I seemed to be good at: lying. "Yeah, really great." *Please don't make it "even better."*

"How good were those munchies. I could go another tray of those quiches."

I smiled. "Agreed." *So far the food had been the best part of the night. Gah, stop complaining, Avery. You need to make the most of it. Have fun.* "What work do you do?"

"I'm a groundskeeper at a golf course." He chuckled, then looked around. "Man, I'm hungry."

I looked at him more closely. His bloodshot eyes weren't half closed, but they weren't fully open either. Okay, so I knew that look. Brad's friends took all sorts of drugs; even Brad smoked weed every now and then, but I didn't want to—I only had one brain, and I wasn't risking it. With my luck, I'd be the one who ended up with a mental illness because of it. Then I laughed because this was funny. It was like a lucky dip of what's wrong with my date now? Seriously. "Are you stoned?"

"Yeah, man. Had a stressful day. One my mates was arrested the other day, and I don't think he did the crime, you know?" He squinted at me. "Hey, are you the reporter who interviewed Donigal's old lady?"

Hmm, maybe this guy would turn out to be an awesome date. "Yes, I am. Are you a friend of Alfie's?"

"Yeah." He shook his head. "The poor guy. He just tries to do the right thing, you know? He's so unlucky."

"What do you mean?"

"He works hard for that lot, and they fired him."

"I heard that they're short of money."

He looked around, then lowered his voice. He leaned forward, but unlike the last guy who did that, I leaned forward too—I had a feeling whatever he was going to say was impor-tant. "Promise not to tell anyone?"

"Of course." In this moment, I meant it. If the informa-tion turned out to be important to the case, I might say some-thing if I knew it wouldn't incriminate this guy. He could be a silent informant.

"I haven't told anyone this, but I'm busting. I feel like it might be my fault he's in jail, and, well, you look like someone who's good at listening. You seem nice."

I smiled because it was a genuine compliment. "Thanks.

I'm mostly nice, and I do like listening, so please, tell me. I promise I won't say anything to anyone."

His voice was even lower, and I had to strain to hear over all the background chatter and laughter. "We both like to smoke… you know."

"Yes." I hoped that their enjoyment of marijuana wasn't the secret.

"Well, I put him in touch with my supplier, and they were looking at a place to grow some product. They talked Alfie into introducing them to Donigal…. Alfie's a great guy, but he's naïve. So many people take advantage of him. He has a good heart." He shook his head slowly. "In any case, Donigal lost it. He told the guy if he ever showed up on the farm again, he'd call the police, and he ended up firing Alfie."

My mouth dropped open. Oh. My. Lord. "Do you think the drug guys did it?"

"All I know is that Alfie would never. I bet that guy is dead. And it's all my fault for introducing them." He sat back, looked down at the table, and picked up a soggy cardboard coaster, then proceeded to tear it into little pieces. Ah, poo on a shoe. This wasn't good.

"I don't suppose you'd tell me the name of the drug guy?"

His head shot up, and he stared at me, fear in his eyes. "No way. I've made enough of a mess for Alfie. I don't want to get either of us killed, thanks. Do you really want to die this young?"

"I suppose not." I wasn't scared of anyone when I was doing my job. Besides, dying wasn't as much of a mystery as it used to be, and even though I wasn't exactly looking forward to it, it wasn't the horror I used to think it was. If I scared easily, I wouldn't be doing this job. You needed a certain amount of an up-yours attitude when investigating criminals, even for a story. Truth and justice were more important. If everyone feared the potential repercussions of finding the hard answers, no one would be in law enforcement, law, or journalism.

Meg rang the bell, and for the first time, I wished the date could go longer.

"It was nice to meet you, Mark. And your secret is safe with me." And I meant it. I'd find some way to look into that without telling Finn because he'd likely freak and go to Bellamy because drug lords did kill people. The only thing that I couldn't quite understand about that angle was that if they went around and asked different farmers, and they all said, no, did they just kill everyone? I thought not. So, what was it about this deal that made them kill Donigal, if, indeed, they were the ones who killed him?

The next three dates were pleasantly average. The guys were fairly normal, inoffensive, and I even laughed a couple of times.

But now it was last-date time.

Finn, tall, dark, and way-too handsome, sat himself in the chair opposite me and smirked. "Ready for the best date of the night, Lightning?"

I grinned. "Are you ready for the most reliable woman in the room, Vinegar?"

He threw his head back and laughed. I couldn't help but join in. When he was done, he looked at me, his blue eyes mesmerizing in the low pub light. Damn him for being so good-looking. My stomach somersaulted, but I ignored it. Okay, I *tried* to ignore it, but it wasn't easy.

Time to kill the mood. "So, what did you find out when you saw your friend today?" I figured keeping this conversation as vague as possible when we were surrounded by locals was the way to go.

Yep, total mood killer. Finn's smile fell, and he gave me a regretful look. "Not great. I'm sure he's innocent though. He's not a liar, and I can tell when people are blagging me. He's depressed. I would be too if I was looking down the barrel of years and years in prison."

Sadness swamped the remnants of my good mood. "I'm sorry. I can't imagine what he's going through. Was he at least happy to see you?"

He rubbed his forehead. "Yeah, he was happy to see me, but when I left, the way he looked at me…. I'm worried about him. He's not coping. We have to find out what happened."

"I'm working on it." I took a deep breath. "If he didn't do it, there must be a clue somewhere—we just haven't found it yet." Justice and truth. It was close to the time where I needed to take a risk. It was time to have another chat with Charles. I'd call him when I got home.

Finn's mouth relaxed into a small smile. "Wanna blow this joint?"

I grinned. "God, yes. Let's go."

As we made our way to the door, everyone stared at us. We waved at Meg who gave us a surprised look. I figured I better text her so she didn't think we were running off to, I don't know, hook up. *We're over it. Going home to our own houses. I don't want to give my number to anyone. Will talk to you tomoz.* I pressed Send as we stepped outside.

"Now I can talk to you properly," Finn said. A gentle breeze blew, which was pleasant in the warm night. The main street wasn't dead, but it was a lot quieter than during the day when all the shops were open. The faded light enhanced the prettiness of the old buildings. Everything seemed so hushed.

"He wouldn't tell me anything, but I think he knows who might have done it."

My eyes widened. He must know he had to keep his mouth shut. To say something or not? *You promised not to.* Whatever I did, it had to be carefully, or I could end up getting two people killed. "Why do you think that?"

"He almost told me something a couple of times, but then shut his mouth. When I asked what, the way he looked at me…. He knew, and he was scared. I'm sure of it. My journalist gut doesn't often steer me wrong. You know what I'm talking about."

I swallowed. "Yeah. You need to trust it. So, what now?"

"Didn't you say you had a lead you were chasing up?"

"I do. I have to talk to my source, but I want to check the farm. The body could be buried there."

He stopped walking and grabbed my arm, turning me to face him. "What do you mean *body*? We can assume, but you say it like it's a done deal. What the heck do you know?"

My heart raced, and I wasn't sure if it was from him holding my arm and staring into my eyes, or that I could get into a lot of trouble if anyone thought I was in on anything, or knew about it without saying anything. Finn would totally run to Bellamy and rat me out. I wasn't stupid—I was the new chick on the block, and Bellamy was an old family friend. Loyalty was what it was. "I don't know for sure." He let go of my arm. "It's a hypothesis we've been discussing based on what he knows. And before you ask, he didn't see what happened, but he saw… something that night."

"Where? Don't be so vague. You promised we would work on this together."

"He saw Donigal's car at the farm after the pub."

"He what?!" His voice was loud enough that a guy walking across the road stared at us.

"Shhhhhh. Anyway, I can't say any more. I promised." Okay, so that was a lie, but it was close to the truth. His body had been there—dead or alive. Whatever... it gave me an excuse to want to search the farm, and that's all I needed right now. Even if he said something to Bellamy, they couldn't prove or disprove it. They could assume my informant lied, for all I cared. "Come on." I started walking, not wanting to cause a scene. Someone was probably already telling someone else they saw Finn and the new girl in town arguing. I could do without that attention.

Finn easily caught up to me with his longer legs. "How long have you known this?"

"The last day or so, and before you get all shouty again, I was trying to figure out what to do with that information. I promised I wouldn't tell the police—my informant doesn't want to be implicated, and I know he didn't do it."

He gave me an incredulous look. "If he was there, he's a suspect. How would you know he didn't do it?"

*Because he's a ghost.* Yeah, that would go down really well. "I trust him."

"Are you dating him?"

"What? I'm not dating anyone. I'm happily single, thank you very much. Men are a double-decker busload of trouble I don't need. The relationship with my ex was enough to scar me for a lifetime. Why would I want to put myself at someone else's mercy again?"

His disbelieving expression turned into something resembling sympathy. "Sorry. I'm making accusations I shouldn't be. I'll just have to trust you. But please, if you learn of anything else, tell me straight away. I won't go running to Bellamy. I would never put you in that situation when you're trying to help my friend."

Silly me wanted to believe him, but smart me took it with a grain of salt. I could trust him only so far. "If I think it will help, I'll definitely tell you."

His forehead scrunched, the deep lines only partly visible through the long fringe that swept from one side to the other. "What else are you hiding from me?"

"Nothing. Look, do you want to search the farm or not? I was going to talk to my source tonight, see if we can narrow down where he might be buried... if he's buried there. I think we can rule out the bits I saw when I was reporting, which was the parking area, front of the house, and the barn near the house."

"Do you know how big that place is? That leaves a lot of acres to cover."

We turned the corner into our street and started up the gradual incline. "Which is why I'm going to talk to my friend first."

"Oh, he's your friend now."

I rolled my eyes. "Source, friend, whatever. Seriously, what does it matter? It's someone I trust, but I'm not dating or intending to ever date. We have quite a big age gap, if you want to know. He's not strong enough to kill someone and drag the body somewhere or dig a hole." He'll probably think he's an old man, which would suit me just fine.

"Do you promise?"

I stopped, and he did the same. I looked into his eyes, throwing as much truth into my gaze as I could. "Yes, I promise. He's trustworthy, he couldn't have done it, and I will never ever date him." The last thing I needed was for him to think there was a conflict of interest.

His shoulders sagged. "Fine." He ran a hand through his hair. We started walking again. Finally, we reached the front fence that ran along both properties. "If you find out anything tonight, can you call me straight away? If we could find a body, the police would have more evidence, and Alfie would have a better chance of getting off."

"I know. I promise I'll call you. If you don't hear from me, it's because my contact has nothing right now, but I'll push him. Okay?"

He took a deep breath. "Okay. I'll see you tomorrow, Lightning."

"Night, Vinegar."

We went our separate ways, and once I was safely in my apartment, I realised something—I would much have rather been here with Finn. I slapped myself across the cheek.

Laughter came from behind me. I turned, and Everly shook her head. "What in God's name are you doing?"

"Reminding myself not to be an idiot. How are you? You've hardly been around lately."

Her chest rose and fell with a large breath… even though she didn't need to breathe. "There's been a lot of ghosts in crisis lately. I don't know what's going on. Whatever it is, it's been keeping me busy. How are you going?" She came over and sat on the couch. I sat next to her.

"Oh, you know, just trying to solve another murder without letting on that I can see ghosts."

She waved a dismissive hand. "Meh, you got this. I have total faith in you. So do a lot of ghosts."

I stared at her. "What do you mean?"

"I know you had a visit from Cathy. Word's getting around about you, Avery—the living person who can see ghosts and wants to help them. I wouldn't be surprised if you start getting ghosts coming from out of area."

"Please, no. I have enough to deal with right now. And how do you know Cathy?"

"She needs to pass, and we were working on some things she couldn't let go of, and this is the last piece of the puzzle for her. When you've done what she's asked you to, she should be able to leave."

I blinked. "*You* recommended me to her?!"

She smiled. "Yes, I did, and it was the right thing to do." She held her wrist up and looked at it, even though she wasn't wearing a watch. "Oh, look at the time. Must go. Bye!" She vanished.

Seriously? Argh! And to think I initially considered that the ghosts would generally leave me alone and my life would be fairly normal. How wrong I'd been. At least I knew I wasn't crazy. That would've been a harder burden to drag around. Speaking of ghosts, I called out, "Charles."

He appeared straight away. Yay. "Hey, Avery. What's up?"

"Any news?"

"The police brought Mrs Donigal in for questioning today and asked her about Alfie being fired. She said they didn't have enough income and that he wasn't pulling his weight. She also told them that Alfie was sometimes aggressive at work when they asked him to do certain jobs, like muck out the horse stalls."

"Really? Did you ever see that?"

His top lip hitched up on one side in dismissal. "Nah. But I only saw him muck out the stalls a couple of times, so who knows? I did see him get angry once with the tractor. He was trying to get it to work, and it wouldn't, and he threw a wrench at the floor. He swore a lot too."

"Okay." I got my notebook out of my bag and wrote everything down. "I have a favour to ask for when it's daylight."

"Yes?"

"Can you do a flyover of Donigal's farm and look for a mound covered with newly dug dirt? If you find one, I need you to describe the location because Finn and I need to find the body, and I have a feeling that it's buried on the farm. If those drug guys killed him and framed Al—"

"What drug guys?"

"Ah, a new angle I'm checking out. Long story, but anyway, if the drug guys killed him and framed Alfie, they probably buried the body on the farm. That way, there would be less evidence than moving him and potentially being caught by police with a body in their boot."

"And if I can't find anything?"

I shrugged. "Then I have to rethink my theory. But if you do find something, I'm going to need to find it, too, so I can tell Bellamy. I have a feeling that if we find the body, there will be evidence that clears Alfie…. At least, that's the hope."

"Okay. But if I'm there, I can't be at the police station to see whoever else they interview."

I would've patted his hand or something, but, well, you know. "That's fine, Charles. This is more important right now. You know, what you've been doing for me and Alfie is fantastic. You've come a long way in the last few weeks."

He looked at me for a moment, his young forehead wrinkled. Then his forehead smoothed, and he smiled. "And it's all because of you. Thank you for helping me."

My eyes burned unexpectedly, but I blinked the tears back —how embarrassing. "It was my pleasure. You're an awesome person. I love seeing you happy."

"And I like seeing you happy, so I'll look for that grave tomorrow and let you know as soon as I'm done."

"Thank you. You're the best."

"Is there anything else?"

"Nope. Thanks. Have a good night."

"You too, Avery." He waved and disappeared.

I texted Finn. Spoke to my guy. *He's checking it out. I'll let you know when he gets back to me. Hopefully before tomorrow afternoon.* It shouldn't take Charles too long since he could be like a drone and look from a height. If I had the funds, I would've bought a drone. I could've even tried to talk Finn into getting one. Then he could've done a flyover of the farm and given me a real-world reason for how we found the grave… if there was one to find. *Now you think of it, Avery, after you've texted Finn. What am I going to do with you?* It was too late now, but next time we needed a visual on something outside, I'd suggest it.

*Thanks, Lightning. Talk to you tomorrow. Sleep well.* The sleep well part of the message gave me more warm and fuzzies than it should have. Reality check—he's just being nice, like he'd be to anyone.

*You too. Night.* I sent the message, then got ready for bed. It had been a loooooong day, and tomorrow might be longer if Finn and I had to go traipsing all over the farm at night.

Turns out, if I'd had an idea of how the day was going to turn out, I might have aborted our plans. I could see ghosts, but, alas, I couldn't tell the future.

# CHAPTER 9

I'd not one minute ago stepped out the front door, and my phone rang. I answered it as I walked to the laneway. "Hello, Avery speaking."

"Avery, this is Sergeant Bellamy." My stomach somersaulted. *Please don't be about that emergency call.* "Are you busy at the moment?"

I stopped walking when I reached my car because I had the unfortunate feeling that I might need it. "Just walking to work."

"If you have time right now, I'd like to see you in my office. It's important." His serious tone didn't make me think he wanted to give me information for my article. He sounded… displeased.

"Of course. I should be there soon. Bye."

He hung up without another word. I took a deep breath, then got in the car and had a small freak-out the entire way to the station. Was it about that call? Was I going to be named as a suspect? Would I end up in a cell? Should I stop and buy him a tart?

*Deep breaths, woman. Think.*

Right, my plan was to deny everything unless he showed me proof. I was sure I'd made my number silent. They couldn't have traced me, surely. *But did you really?* the small voice in my head that loved to push me off balance asked. That voice was the echo of my parents and Brad. They'd left their mark, and I didn't know if I'd ever get rid of it.

When I pulled into the police parking lot, lo and behold, Finn's car was there. At least I thought it was his. I'd never taken notice of his number plate, and his car had been gone this morning, but there were plenty of cars like that, so…. If it was his, why would Bellamy have called us both in? Oh. The farm-supply store. Well, I guessed we both knew this might happen when we went in there. If I had a choice between getting in trouble for the shop thing or the phone call, I'd take the shop every time.

I took my knapsack inside with me. I was well aware of the irony of having something stolen from my car when parked at the police station, but keeping in mind the dodgy people who were coming in and out of there on a regular basis, could you blame me?

PC Adams was at the front desk. She smiled at me. "Hello, Miss Winters. What are you here for?" Did that mean he wasn't livid since he hadn't told everyone about what I'd done wrong?

I smiled. Might as well feign innocence from the get-go. "Hello, PC Adams. Sergeant Bellamy wanted to have a word. I think it's about the Donigal case."

"Righto. I'll let him know you're here." She picked up her

phone and notified him, then hung up. "Just go straight through."

"Thanks." The door buzzed, and I pushed it and went through. Bellamy had sounded annoyed rather than livid when he called, so hopefully it wouldn't be that bad. *You tell yourself that, possum.*

I pretended to be brave as I walked past the officers at their desks—it felt like a walk of shame, but I kept my head held high, and I gave them all a nod of greeting as I hurried past.

Bellamy's door was shut, so I knocked. "Come in." I opened the door. As I suspected, Finn was sitting in one of the chairs on my side of the desk. Bellamy stood. "I'm glad I can do this while you're both here. I'd hate to have to say this all twice." Yikes. He wore his serious-policeman face. "Please sit."

Sergeant Fox stood behind Bellamy's chair. With his of-his-time slicked-back wavy hair and hands resting together behind his back, he said, "Hello, Avery."

I gave him a subtle nod, something no one else would notice. Would the day ever come when I could just put it all out there? Would Bellamy believe me or cart me off to the local hospital? Imagine if he believed. He might want to chat to Fox. Now, that would be a conversation to listen in on.

"So, why are we here?" I asked. If Bellamy had wanted to make us wait and squirm, well, I had news for him. Rip the Band-Aid off, please.

His gaze rested on me, then slid across to Finn. Disappointment weighed heavily in that stare. *Don't roll your eyes, Avery.* He was playing the intimidation game, but it didn't work on me because I knew that's what he was doing. If he didn't say anything soon, I was liable to laugh, and that, I was sure, would not be received well. Rather than roll my eyes, I stared at the ceiling. *Ah, that was better.* Urge relieved. It was almost as good as finally going to the toilet after you were busting.

Finally, his mouth opened, his question directed at Finn. "I have security video of you at a farm-supply store. I thought I told you to stay out of this investigation?"

Finn glanced at me, and I shrugged. "Say whatever you want. I'm with you all the way." I wasn't sure exactly how he wanted to play this, but I'd let him decide since he knew Bellamy better.

"Have you spoken to Tom?"

"You could say that."

"What did he say?"

"Something to the effect that you promised to pay your *father's* debt, *Mr Donigal.*" Okay, so he knew the whole story. Well, he wouldn't be a doing a very good job if he didn't.

Finn folded his arms, the expression on his face defiant. "I know you asked me to stay out of it, but I'm a journalist, and I smell a story... and not the obvious one. There's something else going on here. Have you looked into Donigal's finances?"

"We've looked at everything we need to look at."

"But you're not telling me anything?"

"Not in this instance, no. You have a player in the game, and it's unethical of me." He leaned back and rested his hands on the chair arms.

Finn pressed his lips together in what looked like frustration. I didn't want him getting in trouble, so I jumped in. "You don't have to tell us anything, but if he has money problems, anyone could've killed him to take what they're owed. I happen to know he owes money to more than that vendor."

"Who?" He leaned forward and put his hands on his desk.

"I can't say. I promised." Either I'd annoy a compromise out of him..., or I'd just annoy him.

"I can have you charged for lying to obtain private information. Tell me who else he owed money to, and I'll let it go."

I was pretty sure that lying to obtain private information wouldn't land us in gaol—he might even be overstating things too. It was a small-fry crime, a grey area, and considering our motive was to help get to the truth as journalists, most judges would probably go easy, if it even got that far. It wasn't like we obtained financial benefit from finding out that information. I was calling his bluff. "No. I can't. My word is important to me. Plus, the person who told me is the type of person who might hurt me later."

"Did the person threaten you?"

"Not in so many words, but it was implied."

He pressed his lips together, then looked at Finn. "What are you trying to do? I know you don't think Alfie did it, but you're not thinking straight, son."

Finn shut his eyes as if summoning patience, then opened them again. "I know my friend. He was telling the truth when he said he didn't do it. I'm sure of it. Why haven't you looked at all the other evidence?"

"How do you know we haven't?" We didn't, but we had a good idea. And if my other interactions with this station was concerned, they didn't always get it right.

"Because you would've looked into who else might have wanted to kill Mr Donigal, and it would've led you where it led us."

Fox raised a brow and gave me a stern look. He probably didn't like that I was giving a member of his profession a hard time. Bellamy rested his elbows on the table and steepled his fingers together. "We're privy to information you don't have. We've questioned members of his family, his bank manager, and other associates. We have evidence that will stand up in court. You're asking me to ignore all that and go with what you want, based on what?"

Well, when he put it like that…. I looked at Finn. Alfie was so scre—

"What about gut feeling?" Finn asked.

"My gut tells me that we have enough evidence and a whole lot of other crimes to solve and not enough resources to waste time on a done deal. And if you're not willing to tell me who this other person is, well, there's not much else I can do. Now, as I've asked already, Finn, leave this alone." Argh, this wasn't going well. Maybe we should just apologise and lie about not doing anything else. We didn't have time to waste either.

Someone rapped loudly on his door. Bellamy's chest puffed up with a huge breath, and his jaw muscles bunched. A frustrated "Come in," flew out.

The door opened, and PC Patel—one of the police who'd come to my flat for the rat incident—came in. He ignored Finn and me. "We have a *situation*, Sir." He gave Bellamy a meaningful look.

I stared at Fox and gave him one too. Not sure if he would understand my meaning, I risked looking like a crazy person, and said, "What's going on? I'd love to know." Finn looked at me his gaze incredulous, but then he grinned wryly.

Patel, on the other hand, gave me a "you must be mad" look and turned back to Bellamy. Fortunately, Fox disappeared. Thank you, Sergeant Fox. Bellamy stood. He looked down at me. "You really have no boundaries, do you, Ms Winters?"

"Depends on the circumstances. I'm a journalist—I'm supposed to ask questions."

He rolled his eyes. "Right, time for you two to go, and don't make me have to call you in here again." He stared at

Finn. "Stay out of it. One of these days, you're going to get in the middle of something you can't get out of, and I don't want to have to be the one who calls your father and tells him his son is deceased. Got it?"

Finn stood. Bellamy's words weren't enough to banish the frustrated look on Finn's face. Finn looked at me. "Let's go, Lightning." Without saying goodbye, Finn walked out the door.

I stood and looked at Bellamy. "This means a lot to him, Sergeant, and not to be rude, but you guys don't always get it right. Have a good afternoon." Okay, so while I'd been thinking that, I wasn't supposed to say it. But maybe it needed to be said. I walked out, leaving Patel and Bellamy staring at me, their mouths hanging open.

Finn stood just outside the door, his eyes wide. He stared at me for a moment, then chuckled. "Well, aren't you full of surprises. Come on."

I followed him to the corridor, then grabbed his arm, stopping him. "Just wait here for a sec. See where they're going, or if they say anything about what's going on."

His brow wrinkled. "Why do you care? It's probably nothing we need to know about. Are you short on stories or something?"

"No. I have a bad feeling. If it was something happening outside the station, they'd deal with it themselves or call him. I have a feeling something's going on here, which could be Alfie. He's still locked up here, isn't he?"

Finn paled. "You're right."

We peeked around the corner. Bellamy was punching in the code at the door that, presumably, led to the cells. He pulled it open, and they both ran in. Fox appeared in front of me, and I started.

Finn gave me a worried look. "Are you okay?"

"Ah, yeah, just had sharp pain in my stomach. I think maybe breakfast isn't agreeing with me." Once Finn's gaze hit the door again, I glanced at Fox and mouthed, "What happened?"

"Alfie tried to hang himself, but he wasn't successful. They'll have to put him on suicide watch now."

Oh my God. My stomach fell. I swallowed and mouthed, "Thank you."

"All good. I have to say though, I thought he had done it. I've been humouring you, keeping Charles around. But now I'm not so sure our prisoner is guilty. Good luck, Avery."

I gave him a nod of thanks because Finn was turning towards me. "How are we going to find out what's going on?"

The exit door at the other end of the corridor burst open, and paramedics rushed through. Finn and I stepped into the office area to get out of the way. We looked at each other. "I don't mind getting in trouble," I said. "I'll go look." I wouldn't even have to go look. If I could get into the next section, I could just stand inside the door for a few moments, then I could come back and tell him what I already knew.

"Okay, but be careful."

I nodded. "Gotta go."

While the paramedics waited at the door, I dropped to the floor and crawled between desks, stopping behind the desk closest to the door. When Patel opened it to let the paramedics through, he stepped back, then led the way. I hurried to the closing door on all fours, and just before it shut, I stopped it and waited, my heart racing. If they saw me, I doubt I'd get arrested, but I could get in trouble and be banned from the station, all my goodwill with Bellamy destroyed, but to ease

Finn's mind without explaining that I could see ghosts was worth it.

I counted to five, then opened the door. The hallway was empty, and footsteps clattered along the hall from around the corner. I crawled in and let the door shut almost closed so it would look to Finn as if it was. I looked up. Just as I'd thought —there was another keypad on the door to get out. I'd be locked in. My heartbeat thundering in my ears, I waited, and waited, and waited. Muffled voices came from somewhere inside the cells. I stared at the corner, expecting someone to walk into the corridor at any second. This was excitement I didn't need.

After counting out two minutes—sufficient time for Finn to think I'd gone all the way in and listened—I pushed the door open, then let it close behind me. I stood and jogged to where he waited. "Alfie tried to hang himself, but they got to him in time. He's going to be okay." Finn's expression froze. He stayed like that for a bit, until I couldn't wait any longer. "We need to leave before they come out. Come on."

His eyes regained focus, and he looked at me. "Are you sure? Are you sure he's not dead?"

Fox appeared and gave me a nod. "He's okay. They're going to take him to hospital for overnight observation; then he'll be moved to a facility where he can be watched more closely."

"Yes. I'm positive. "They're going to take him to hospital to make sure, so we need to leave before they wheel him out."

"No, we don't. I want to wait in the car park and see. There's a side entrance to the cells too. If you watch the entrance and I watch the side, we can make sure he's okay."

I huffed. "Fine, don't believe me. Let's go."

I waved to PC Adams as we hurried out to the car park.

Once out there, I stayed near the door and watched that exit. Finn left and went to the left of the building and disappeared around the corner. The ambulance was parked near my entrance—because that's where they'd come in.

Shortly, I heard rattling. The paramedics appeared from around the corner, pushing a bed with their patient strapped in. PC Patel was with them, as was Finn. He was hurrying alongside the bed. "It's okay, Alfie. Everything's going to be okay." Alfie stared at the sky, leaving Finn's comments unacknowledged. He wasn't in a good way at all.

They put him in the back of the ambulance. Finn stood and watched, helpless, as they shut the ambulance doors. Patel got in a police car, and when the ambulance left, he followed them, leaving Finn forlornly standing there alone. That was the only thing I could fix right now, so I went to him.

"Hey, are you okay?"

He looked at me, his eyes filled with despair. "I failed him."

I sucked my bottom lip into my mouth. Seeing people sad set all my empathy alarms off. I wanted to hug and comfort him, but it might be taken the wrong way, so I abstained. The best I could do was use a kind voice and pretend everything was going to be fine. "We'll get to the bottom of this. I promise."

Two divots appeared above the bridge of his nose. "I appreciate the sentiment, but that's a promise you can't make."

His comment would've upset me, except he was right.

# CHAPTER 10

After that depressing turn of events, I went and covered a story I'd booked last week. Once I'd done that, I returned to the office to write the article. After this morning's depressing scene, I desperately wanted Charles to come through with something, and waiting for that to happen was torturous. I needed to keep busy and distracted, so I wandered to the pub. Might as well fill Meg in on what'd been going on. I found her behind the bar, Bailey nowhere in sight.

"Avery! What brings you here before lunch?"

"Killing time, to be honest. Thought you might like to know about my morning with Vinegar."

She chuckled as she always did when I mentioned his nickname. "What happened?"

I told her about being summoned by Bellamy and swore her to secrecy about Alfie. "Well, you can tell Bailey but no one else, and you have to swear him to secrecy. I doubt Alfie will want everyone to know his personal business, but I know you guys like him. Maybe you could see if they'll allow visitors eventually?"

"Yeah, that's a good idea, but, honestly, I'm sad." She shook her head. "I can't believe he could kill anyone. What does your gut tell you? You've already solved two crimes since coming here. Do you think you can make it three from three?"

"I'm doing my best, trust me. This one's tricky though. Everyone who's given me information has sworn me to secrecy, and if I told Bellamy what I know, everyone would know it was me who gave it up."

"But isn't the truth more important?"

"In this case, it could potentially lead to more murder— mine and someone else's. I'm not willing to risk it yet. I have one more thing up my sleeve. If this doesn't pan out, I'll have to resort to going back on my word. It's a total last resort though."

She rubbed her lips. "Wow, that's heavy."

"Tell me about it." I sighed. "Anyway, just wanted to update you rather than be a mood killer. How did last night end up? Did you raise much money?"

She smiled. "Yes! It was a great success. Thanks for coming. Have you written your story on it yet?"

"Ah, no. I will though. I'm trying to keep busy today, but it's the kind of article you need to be in a good mood to write. I don't want it to come across as too snarky."

"Oh, did you have some terrible dates?"

I gave her a deadpan look. "Terrible is too mild a term. The best date was Vinegar, so that tells you how well it went."

She laughed. "And you two scooted off early. Bailey didn't look too enthused about that."

I smiled. What? Okay, so I was avoiding dating, but I could be happy that he was a bit sad that I left with another guy.

Moving right along. "We were talking work. Nothing happened—nothing will ever happen. As soon as we got to our front fence, he went to his place, and I went to mine. There was no touching, no pining gazes, etc. He's a player, and I have to work with him. It's never going to happen."

She gave me an assessing look. "Hmm, that's what they all say."

Time for a subject change. "I reckon Luke fancies you." I waggled my brows.

It was her turn to fight a smile. The smile won. "You think?" She waved her hand. "Meh, it doesn't even matter. Chris and I aren't doing too badly at this long-distance thing. I'm taking a couple of days off next week and going up to see him."

I smiled. "That's great."

"Meg, darling, did you order that—" Meg's dad walked in and stopped when he saw we were talking. "Hello, Avery. Solving any murders lately?"

I laughed. "Trying to at the moment…. Well, it's a suspected murder anyway. How have you been?"

"Good, good. I don't know how I ever thought the kids could handle this place by themselves. It's seven days a week, and they need a life too. I'm going to get more involved on a permanent basis again." He put his hands on his hips and looked around before resting his gaze on Meg. "I missed the kids too. This is where I belong."

Meg smiled. "We missed you too, and I won't lie—having another pair of hands around here is more than welcome."

"Oh, and you put that new bloke on," I pointed out. Maybe this meant Meg and I could have more nights out, maybe go to Exeter or somewhere further afield. I really hadn't done much exploring since I'd gotten here because I'd been so keen to settle in and do well at work.

"He's going well so far," Meg said. "We're doing enough trade that we could afford it. It's a relief to be honest."

Her dad nodded. "You and Bailey have done an incredible job with this place, love."

How nice that they were getting along so well. Seeing a functional family interact proved to me that it was possible. I'd just lost the lottery in that respect, but it didn't mean that maybe one day that I couldn't create my own family. If I ever had kids—although the idea still scared the hades out of me—I'd love them, be there for them, and teach them to be empathetic, kind, and logical. I'd also teach them how to play Scrabble because no one ever wanted to play with me.

"Avery."

I almost turned at the call, but at the last second my brain computed that it was Charles's voice. Oh my goodness—he must have information. I swallowed the mixture of terror and excitement. *Please be the news I was waiting for.* Then my phone rang. Seriously? "I guess I'd better go. I've got a fair bit on this afternoon. See you later."

"Bye, Avery." Meg waved.

"Don't be a stranger," her dad said. Well, that was nice and unexpected. When we first met, he was wary, but he must've figured out that I wasn't a danger to Meg.

I hurried outside and answered my phone. "Hey, Vinegar. I was just about to talk to my guy." I turned and Charles had followed me out. He stopped next to me and folded his arms. I mouthed, "Sorry."

"Hey. I have information on Field. I called in a favour. Meet me at the office ASAP. Where are you, by the way?"

"I'm just at the pub. I'll chat to my guy, then I'll come straight over. Be there in five."

"Can't wait to hear if you've got any news. What I have is huge." By the excitement in his voice, this was going to be good for Alfie.

"Now you're leaving me in suspense. Argh! See you soon. Bye."

"Bye."

I kept my phone where it was. "Sorry about that. So, what did you discover? Please tell me you found the body." *Please be the breakthrough we need.*

"I saw a mound in a field that's lying fallow. There's long grass, but from above, it's easy to see the different colour of dirt. I don't know if it's a grave, but it's the right size I think."

I wanted to get excited, but if it wasn't his body, it would be too crushing, so I took a couple of slow breaths. "Can you describe where it is?"

He cocked his head to one side and looked in the opposite direction. "Hmm." He met my gaze. "It's not near the house. It's in a back field."

"North of the house, south, east?"

"I have no idea." He scratched the end of his nose.

"What if I showed the farm to you on a map?"

"Yeah, that could work."

I smiled. "Great." My shoulders sagged. "But I have to go straight to the office. Maybe come with and I'll pull it up. I won't be able to acknowledge what you tell me because Finn's there, but point where you think it was on the screen, and before we go tonight, I'll call you when I'm home by myself to ask a few more questions about fences and gates and stuff."

"Oh, I don't know if I can remember all that." Worry radiated from his eyes.

"It's okay. Maybe we'll take wire cutters or something. We'll go prepared for any eventuality. Thank you so much, Charles. You've done an outstanding job."

"Thanks, but just wait till you see what it is. Maybe I just found a mound of dirt."

I started walking. "I won't get my hopes up, but I won't assume it's nothing either."

Before long, we were back at the office. Carina and Finn were at their desks. As much as Carina wanted to be in the loop, Finn and I hadn't discussed letting her in on us going to the farm. We would be trespassing, which was illegal. Would she want to know about that? Would she feel compelled to tell Bellamy what we were planning? She didn't strike me as that kind of person, someone who was hell-bent on doing the legal thing even if it was for the greater good to break the rules a bit.

"Hey, you two."

"Avery, girl. How're you going?" Carina smiled.

"Good thanks. Finn has some news, apparently." I looked at him. "Tell me. I'm dying to know." Charles sat on the spare desk that was behind mine. Ah, that's right. I could set up my laptop while Finn talked. I sat.

"Okay, so I had a friend look into Mr Field. There's a good reason he doesn't want anyone to know who he really is." He took out a notebook and opened it.

Carina leaned forward. "Ooh, I love a good secret."

I stopped what I was doing and stared at Finn. I didn't want to miss a word of this. It's not like we could traipse around the farm in daylight anyway, and Charles could wait five minutes for me to bring up the map. Who knew, maybe he was happy to listen in on our chat since he'd had a lot to do with this case so far.

"His real name is Barnaby Killeen. He spent eight years in prison for attempted murder, during which time his wife left him and took their son." He looked up at me. "And this is the kicker." His gaze found his notebook again. "The person he tried to kill by beating him with a shovel was his neighbour."

My mouth fell open. "Oh. My. God. What?!"

Carina's eyes were wide. "Wow, he could be our man, d'en."

I swallowed. "Well, I'm glad I didn't say anything to Bellamy, but if we find the body, I'll say something then because there could be evidence that helps tie him to it, and then I won't be on the guy's hitlist." Was I wrong on the drug-lord angle? "Why did he try to kill his neighbour?"

"He said he lost it, and he wasn't trying to kill him. The lawyer tried to get the charge reduced to assault, but the judge said no since he bought the shovel that morning. Field... or Killeen I should say, swore that it was just a coincidence. His neighbour was a difficult person, apparently. He had loud parties all the time that went late, had dogs that barked constantly and that got out. One of the dogs bit his son on the leg once, but back then, they didn't put the dogs down."

"Gee, we're talking close to twenty or more years ago. Did he just snap one day?"

"According to Killeen's testimony, he went to the neighbour's to talk to him about fixing the back fence that separated their properties. It was falling down, and he wanted to keep the dogs out. The neighbour refused. The next day, one of the dogs got into Killeen's yard and bit his son. The boy needed twenty stitches and lost a lot of blood. Killeen bought a shovel the next morning and went to visit his neighbour."

"Sounds like d'e judge got it right."

Finn looked at Carina. "Yes, he did." He looked at me.

"It's lucky we didn't say anything to Bellamy yet. This guy is dangerous. Yes, he's older now and might have mellowed, but if he has a temper like that, I'm not surprised he didn't do something to Donigal ages ago when they first had issues."

I cocked my head to the side. "However, his child wasn't involved this time. Some people just lose it when it comes to their kids. And who knows if the neighbour taunted him? Maybe he's not as volatile as this indicates." Finn's expression was disbelieving. "Look, I like to give people the benefit of the doubt, especially when accusing them of murder. The best thing we can do now is find the body."

"Have you had any luck?" Carina asked.

I shared a look with Finn and gave him a small nod. It was his call. He gave a nod back. "I understand Avery has something to share with us right now."

"Right. Well, my source tells me that there is something that looks suspiciously like a freshly covered mound in one of the fallow fields. I'm waiting for the rough location." I went into Google maps and brought up the property. I'd have to go through it with Charles when the conversation was over. "So, we go in tonight, when it's dark. Vinegar and I can do the searching, and I think it would be a great idea to have you as backup at home. If anything goes wrong, and we don't keep up contact, you can notify Bellamy."

"That sounds like a good idea." Finn turned to Carina. "Are you okay with that?"

"Oh, I don't like missing out on d'e action, but if anyone realises you're d'ere, d'ey might just shoot at you, so maybe you do need someone ready to call Bellamy. You know you'll get into trouble about d'e trespassing."

"It can't be helped." Finn put his notebook in his bag. "There's no way Bellamy will search that farm on our say so."

He looked at me. "Before you came, he gave me an earful about Donigal's son. He's not happy that Bellamy brought his mother in for questioning. He says it's given her anxiety. He just wants Alfie put away and for everyone to leave them alone."

I scrunched my face. "Doesn't he want his father found?"

Carina twirled a lock of blue hair in her fingers. "As long as I've been here, the mother's been a bit of a recluse. Even Donigal only comes into town when he has to."

"Carina's right," said Finn. "Before he stopped working the farm with his dad, Danny would come into town for his parents, but after he left to do his own thing, Donigal would come in. Never saw the wife."

I turned to Carina. "Oh, did you find anything out at the craft night?" I knew I'd forgotten something.

"Oh, yes. Mrs Donigal hasn't been the last few weeks. Her hip has been bad, apparently, but the women seem to think it's because her husband won't let her spend money on the wool."

Charles had come to stand next to me. He made gestures for me to move the map to the left and up a bit. I did that. "When I interviewed her, she had a limp. It did look painful, and her house inside is… basic. Everything points to them having no money, but the neighbour says otherwise. Ownership of the farm shows there aren't any loans on it, so I don't know. Do you think the son would talk to us? I saw him in the café the other morning." Charles motioned again, and I moved the map. He peered closer.

"No." The way Finn said that made me think they had history. "Even if he did, he wouldn't tell the truth. He's a show-off. At school, he was always trying to one up everyone. He was a couple of years ahead of me. He used to brag that his farm was the biggest one for miles, and that they were rich."

"Oh." When I thought about it though, he was dressed well at the café and carried himself as if he had money. "So even if he's gone away and made some cash, he'd still be precious about his parents?"

"I'd assume so." Finnegan shut his laptop, then looked at me. "Meet at mine at ten tonight?"

"Sounds good. We might have to do some digging. Have you got a shovel?" I had no idea if Mrs Crabby had one, but there was no way I was borrowing anything of hers. It would just give her an excuse to get angry at me.

"Yes, I have one. Have you got rubber gloves?"

"Yes."

"Bring them. We don't want our DNA to get mixed up with anything, and we might have to dig with our hands."

"As long as I don't have to drag a body anywhere, that's fine."

Carina's mouth made an O. "If d'ere is a body d'ere, you're going to have to see it… and smell it. Are you going to be okay wit' d'at?"

Finn laughed. "Avery's an old hand at finding dead bodies. I'm sure she can give me some tips."

Carina chuckled. "Oh, d'at's right. How could I forget?"

"With Avery's luck at finding dead bodies, I reckon we could find one tonight."

I stared at Finn. "As long as it's the one we want to find, I'll be okay with it. Touch wood." I touched the tabletop. What were the odds that it was someone else's body? Were we about to stumble into another crime? Please no.

"That's it. That's the spot." Charles was pointing at the

screen. I took a screen shot, brought that up, then drew a red dot on it.

"Well, all I know is that I have to thank my contact because he's done a good job so far. Let's hope he's right about what he saw." I glanced at Charles so he wouldn't miss the roundabout way I was trying to thank him.

He smiled. "Thanks, Avery." His smile fell. "I have an icky feeling about this. If it's him, call me as soon as you can. You might be able to try whispering. Sometimes I think it's the energy and intent that sends your voice to me. Anyway, be careful tonight. Bye." I gave a half wave that Carina and Finn couldn't see.

Why would he have an icky feeling? He's already dead. Surely dead bodies didn't bother him.

Finn had packed his stuff away while I'd been lost in thought. "So, Carina will come to my place and wait for us there. If she doesn't get a text from us every thirty minutes, she'll wait an extra ten and text us. If we don't return it, she'll call Bellamy. Make sure your phone is fully charged before you come tonight, Avery."

"Um, will do."

He walked to the door. "Tonight, we'll hopefully get to the bottom of it. I'll see you both later."

After Finn left, Carina stared at me. "I don't know whed'er to be excited or worried."

I knew which one I was, especially after Charles's "icky" comment. But what was the point of stressing Carina when, good or bad, we were definitely doing this? I gave her a fake smile. "I'm excited. And if everything goes well, Alfie will be out of gaol before we know it." I could pretend with other people, but I couldn't ignore the shiver that skittered down my spine.

What were we going to find?

Back at home, I went through the map one more time with Charles because I was paranoid, and I had been a tad distracted at the office. Then I had to force dinner down—my stomach was a roiling mass of misgivings. Was I worried because I could sense something bad coming, or was it just in reaction to Charles's feelings? I'd have to wait till it was too late to find out. Great.

Keeping in mind there would be long grass since the field wasn't being used, and there'd been recent rain, so it would be muddy, I wore black jeans, black long-sleeve top, gumboots, and took a black metal torch, one of those ones you could conk someone over the head with. I could use my phone as a torch, but it could suck battery power quickly, and my phone was more important as a communication device. I got my small, black backpack and put the torch in it, along with rubber gloves, spare batteries for the torch, a bottle of water (because digging up bodies was thirsty work), and a raincoat in case the weather turned dodgy, which was always a possibility in England. I was pretty sure that was everything.

It was nine thirty, but we needed time to discuss how we were getting to that particular field, so I quietly locked my apartment and crept down the stairs. It was way after eight, and if I woke Mrs Crabby, there'd be hell to pay.

Last time I'd gone from my place to his at night was when I was running from a murderer. Probably not a good omen. And it wasn't that long ago. How was this my life? On the positive side, it was better than being locked in a hospital and forced to take meds that turned me into a zombie.

I knocked on his door, and it didn't take long for him to answer. When he opened the door, I laughed. "Twinsies!" He was wearing exactly what I was.

He gave me a "you didn't just say twinsies" look. "It's common sense. Black because it's night, and wellies because we're going to be traipsing through mud and wild fields."

"Thanks for ruining my fun." I went past him into the house and to the living area. He had two black velvet armchairs and a tan leather couch. Last time I'd been here, I'd been rather stressed. Now that I was calmer, I could see that this furniture was expensive. There was also a six-seater antique dining table and timber and cream-fabric dining chairs. An empty black glass vase sat in the middle of the dining table. What sort of guy had a vase on their table?

"Are you going to stand in the doorway all night?"

I started. "Oops, sorry." I hurried to the couch and sat on one side. "So, here's the map. I've marked our destination on it." I got the picture up and handed him the phone. "That's zoomed out. It's so far from the house that I'm hoping there's another way to access it rather than the main driveway. I mean, we could wait till even later to make sure everyone's asleep, but it's risky. They've got a dog."

He examined the image for a couple of minutes. "Hang on." He left the room and soon returned with his laptop. He sat in the middle of the couch. The small gap between us wasn't enough for my liking.

A knock sounded on the front door. I jumped up. "I'll get it. Must be Carina." Newsflash—it was.

When I returned to the living area with her in tow, I sat on one of the single chairs, and Carina took a seat next to Finn. She looked at the screen. "Watcha doin'?

"Just checking out where the fence lines are. This could be a couple of years old, but it should still be the same."

"Oh, do you have bolt cutters or wire cutters or whatever?" That's what I forgot, but to be fair, I didn't want to buy them. I should've remembered to ask Finn to buy some. Judging by his furniture, he had way more money than me.

"I have them in my bag."

Carina patted him on the back. "Finny's a good one to have on your side when you have trespassing to do." She laughed.

"Should we take a sausage or something in case the dog comes after us?" The dog hadn't looked super threatening, but with dogs, you never knew. If it was trained to protect their property, we could be in big trouble.

Finn stared at me. "We're not in a movie. I don't think that would work."

My forehead wrinkled. "Why not? Distractions work. Isn't it better than hurting the dog?"

He gave me a "you've got to be kidding" look. "Avery, we're going to be possibly half a mile or more from the road. You reckon you can outrun a dog over that distance in the dark when there will be dips and long grass, and you're wearing wellies. A dog can scoff a sausage in two seconds flat. It's a waste of time."

I smiled sweetly. "Maybe the dog will be endeared to us if we give it a sausage?" Carina snorted, but Finn kept looking at me like he was dealing with a moron of massive proportions. I rolled my eyes. "Fine, but you can hurt the dog if it attacks us. I don't want to."

He slammed a hand over his eyes before dropping his hand and looking at me. He shook his head as if he couldn't believe what he was about to say and had no idea why he was giving in. "Argh, take a damn sausage, then. In fact, take two. There's some in my fridge." He waved towards the door.

I didn't want to celebrate my win, but I couldn't help the grin that spread across my face. Carina was beaming, and even Finn, despite himself, reluctantly smiled. "Thank you! Thank you!" I didn't mind elbowing human scum in the face, but I drew the line at animals. Obviously if it was a me-or-them scenario, I would save myself, but I would hate myself for it afterwards.

I jumped up and went to his kitchen, which I'd seen last time as well. It was modern, with dark timber-looking cupboards, white-marble benchtops, a gas stove, and two wall ovens. Did he cook, or was this just for looks?

I went to the black double-door fridge and opened the right-hand-side door. The middle shelf held a tub of butter, cheese, eggs, and a plate of four sausages. I grabbed two and wrapped them in the plastic wrap that covered the plate. Lazy, I knew, but I didn't want to hunt around his kitchen for more plastic wrap. I hurried back to the living room and put the puppy snacks in the front zip-up up section by itself.

As I lowered my bum onto the armchair, Finn looked at me. "Come and sit here so you can see the screen. I have a plan."

"Cool." I got up and sat next to him, making sure there was enough gap that we weren't touching, even though I just wanted to snuggle into his side. I was so worried he'd know I was attracted to him that I was going out of my way to ensure he didn't. It was for my own good. "So, what's the plan?"

"You're in luck." Carina pointed to a fence line next to a road. "You can park here—it's about a quarter mile east of the driveway."

Finn pointed at the screen. "See this here? It's the

boundary between Donigal's and Killeen's farms. And if you notice"—he moved the map down on the screen to reveal more of the northern area—"the mound your friend talks about is roughly four hundred feet from that boundary. But since it's all the way up here, we're going to have to navigate roughly half a mile of uneven ground on an incline. It's going to be slow-going."

"Should take you about fifteen minutes. You'll have to cut through the fence along the road, then two other fences along the way." Carina looked at Finn. "Doesn't seem too bad."

"As well as horses, they have a few cows and some sheep, too, don't they?" I asked.

"Yes." Finn looked at me. "Why?"

"I don't want them getting out and getting killed. We have to fix the fence along the road before we leave. Okay?"

He stared at me for a moment, a blank look on his face. Resignation edged into his gaze. "Yes, of course. I should've thought of that. I'll add some plyers to my kit. I have a couple of blocks of wood in the shed. I'll hammer some nails in them, and we can twist the wire around that. It's the best I can do because I don't have fence wire handy, and it has to hold."

"Thanks." I smiled. We were already breaking the law by trespassing, and I didn't want to do any more damage than we absolutely had to.

"So, Avery, you clear on what we're doing?"

"Crystal."

"Good. I'll go sort the wood. Be back in five." Finn left, taking his solid warmth with him.

Carina and I chatted until he got back. When he walked into the room, he carried his knapsack, which was also black like mine. He also held a shovel. My heart rate picked up, and it wasn't because of my Finnegan crush. We were really doing this. Trespassing to search for a dead body. I swallowed and stood. "I guess it's time to go." I looked at Carina. "I'll call you when we get there and text when we're through the first fence. After that, I'll text when we find something. If you haven't heard from me thirty minutes after the first text, text me. If I don't answer, try calling. If that fails, call the police."

She gave a firm nod. "Consider it done." Carina stood and gave me a hug. That was unexpected. "Be careful."

"We will. We'll be fine now we have sausages." I winked.

Carina giggled. "Wield your sausages well, fair maiden."

It was my turn to laugh. "I'm an expert with sausages. Fear not." I snorted. Finn shook his head and laughed. We all said a final goodbye, and I followed Finn outside and down the laneway to his car.

We got in, and neither of us said anything until he had his blinker on to turn right on the main road. "How you feeling?" he asked.

"Nervous... worried... excited that we're about to do something to potentially help Alfie. If I'm honest, sneaking around in the dark is kind of fun... at least the idea of it is. Getting caught won't be."

His tone was all calm determination. "We won't get caught. The only way someone will know we've been there is if we come across a dead body and we call Bellamy." He glanced at me. "Thanks again for doing this. Alfie's struggling. If he kills himself, I'll never forgive myself."

I would've explained that it wouldn't be his fault, but really, there wasn't much to say that could stop his worry. The only thing that would do that was finding the body and being able to prove Alfie was innocent. If Alfie had done it, well, that was something Finn would have to come to terms with. Life was cruel like that. There was some pain we couldn't save ourselves or others from. "Any time. You know I can't pass up a good story or a challenging mystery." Which reminded me—I still hadn't written the dating story. Argh. I was my own worst enemy. I'd get it done tomorrow.

After that, we were quiet for the entire drive. His navigation app told us to pull over—and there it was, the Donigal's closed front gate. Finn looked at the thing on the dash that counted the miles—okay, so I didn't know what it was called, so sue me. When it clicked over the quarter mile, he pulled onto the grass at the side of the road. Luckily there was enough room for his car to fit.

We got out, and I looked up. The cloud was patchy, and the moon about three-quarters full. "Some light, which is good. Means we won't have obvious torchlights bobbing through the field." I breathed out in relief—it also meant we should avoid any storms. If one ambushed us, Finn would be left trying to wrangle a panicking mess. Anger warmed my stomach—I hated being beholden to my PTSD. It was frustrating and embarrassing. Would I ever be free of it?

Finn lifted his shovel out of the boot, then locked the car. I took my torch out of my bag—in case I had to hit something —and made sure my phone was easily accessible in my back jeans pocket. I put my backpack on—extra protection from behind if the dog jumped on me. "Ready to roll?" he asked, his voice quiet and full of tension.

"As I'll ever be. That body won't find itself, so let's go."

He chuckled, which brought the stress level down a couple of notches. "I don't think anyone's ever said that to me before." He pulled the bolt cutters out of his bag, and we went to the fence. Within a minute, he had the top three wires cut, which left only two lower ones that were easy to step over. He grabbed a piece of timber with the nails out of his bag and attached it to the second-top wire. "That should hold if any livestock come this way." He turned and looked up the hill. "If I've read the map right, Killeen's property is just over there." He pointed to our right. "So we need to head up the hill. I've set my GPS tracker, so we know how far we've walked, and I've started us slightly west of where I think the mound will be. That way, we can slowly move towards the fence when we get to the general vicinity. We don't want to be going back and forth because we'll be more likely to miss it."

I texted Carina and put my phone back in my pocket. "Okay. Lead the way."

As we walked, every now and then, he checked his phone, and I wiped sweat off my brow. The night wasn't super hot, but it was still probably twenty degrees Celsius, and with the incline and long sleeves and jeans, it was toasty. After five minutes, I asked, "How far have we gone?"

"Oh, I'm not checking that. I'm using a compass to make sure we don't go off our line. It would be easy to drift one way or the other."

"Fair enough." There was more to this wandering around in a field at night-time than I thought. I listened intently for noises that indicated vicious dogs, people with shotguns, or raging bulls. So far, the only sounds were frogs and the occasional owl hoot. When we reached the second fence, Finn used the bolt cutters, and we quickly continued.

My foot wonked into a hole. I twisted my ankle and stumbled forward, trying not to fall. Pain shot through my ankle and foot. "Ow!" I slammed my hand over my mouth. Possum poo. Was I trying to get found out?

Finn stopped and whispered, "Are you okay?"

I breathed for a moment, assessing. Placing my foot down gingerly, I carefully leaned on it till it took my full weight. I was such a clumsy idiot. "I think I'm fine. Nothing's sprained, just a dull ache. Sorry, I'll be more careful."

He looked at me. "Um, I'm not having a go at you. Just don't break anything. I forgot to bring a sled." He chuckled.

I smiled despite myself. If I ever hurt myself in front of my family or Brad, they'd tell me I was clumsy, stupid, or careless followed by a lecture. Apparently, I was taking up the mantle for them and repeating their criticisms to myself. I needed to work on stopping that. "We'll have to remember one next time."

"Are you good to keep going?" He looked at his phone, shielding the screen from the position of the house, which, if my sense of direction was right, was to the west of us. "We don't have far to go. Maybe a couple of minutes."

I took a couple of steps. "Yep, all good." The clouds had cleared even more, and stars glittered across the vast darkness as we travelled the final few minutes to begin the proper search. Finn surged ahead of me, then stopped. When I reached him and the waist-high pile of firewood he stood next to, he said, "This is it. This is where we start. We'll make our way in that direction. Maybe we should stay about twenty feet apart. Then we'll miss less but still cover the ground we need to. We'll walk all the way to the boundary, then move west again and walk back to be in line with this pile. Pretty handy spot for it, wouldn't you say?"

"Maybe they want to burn the body eventually, or maybe they sometimes have bonfires out here, or maybe it was a tree near this spot, and they couldn't be bothered moving the wood?"

"What, only three suggestions, Lightning?" He chuckled.

"Ha, very funny. Sorry, my brain goes a million miles an hour sometimes. Right, so, let's start." I hoped it didn't take long because the longer it took, the more likely we'd be discovered. Although that was me just being paranoid. The house was so far away that no one in there could hear us, let alone see us.

Finn walked a few lengths away, then turned to the east. I copied him. As we walked slowly, we both looked left and right, scanning our immediate surroundings for what I figured would be a low mound. The grass swished against my legs. I strained my eyes trying to pick things out in the dimness. The moonlight was better than what I expected, but it wasn't super bright. If it got any darker, we'd have to use our torches.

As we neared the fence line, I walked into a cold patch of air. It puckered my skin, just like when ghosts were around. I sucked in a breath and gripped my torch handle tighter. Stopping, I gazed around. "Donigal, are you here?" I whispered. Finn looked towards me—he would've heard me say something. I spoke in a whisper-hiss. "I'm just talking to myself." He nodded. I wasn't worried because it was something you could say out loud and not really mean, like when you look for your sunglasses and say, "Where are you?"

I looked to my right and ahead, then inched my head forward and squinted. One thing I hadn't counted on was because the grass was long, it obscured things close to the ground. I thought I could see a bare patch of raised dirt, but I wasn't sure if it was my eyes making it up out of shadows in the darkness. I pulled my torch out and walked closer.

The temperature dropped further. Yikes. I held my breath and listened as I neared. It was the kind of moment you expected zombies to start jumping out of the ground.

I clicked my torch on, the noise echoing in the dead quiet.

My steps were measured and careful as I approached what was clearly fresh dirt in the midst of long grass now more light shone. I was about to call to Finn, but his footsteps sounded behind me. By the time I reached the human-sized hump, he was next to me. We looked at each other. My heart galloped, and I swallowed. We were potentially about to dig up a dead, rotting body. It wasn't going to be pretty.

I whispered, "I think we dig just enough to confirm it's a body, like till we find a hand or leg or whatever, then we call Bellamy. We don't need to see or smell it."

"But what if it's not Donigal? Don't you want to confirm?"

"Okay, we can do enough to see the face, but I'm warning you, it's going to be beyond gross. I don't even know how this stuff works, but he might have maggots or worms all over him. His face might be bloated so we can't even recognise him." I really didn't want to be here longer than we had to be, and even though I was cool with all the afterlife stuff now, seeing a rotting face would surely give me nightmares.

He walked to one end of the long mound. "I'll start here." He took his backpack off and fished around in it, then held something out. "Here. You can start at the other end." He handed me a trowel.

"Ah, thanks, I guess." I turned my torch off—no point drawing people to us. There was enough light to dig by. I called Carina and filled her in on the situation, and she wished us luck. "I'll call you back as soon as I know more. If I don't call in thirty minutes, call me. This shouldn't take that long."

"Will do, Avery."

I hung up. Then Finn and I put on our gloves and got to work.

Kneeling on the ground, I stuck the trowel into the soil, and my stomach clenched. I wasn't looking forward to the end of it hitting flesh. Ew. How in hades did I ever think this was a good idea? Maybe next time I came up with a brilliant scheme, I should just ignore myself. Up to this point, my decision-making skills hadn't exactly been overly beneficial to me. Maybe I should just run everything by Meg from now on.

The scent of freshly turned soil and cow dung overwhelmed the still air. A breeze would've been nice about now. The crisp *chck* of Finn's shovel strokes cutting into the earth gave me a rhythm to work to. It was better to focus on that than what potentially lay underneath.

Which one of us would make the discovery? My money was on Finn since he was working with a bigger implement.

*Chck, thud.*

I gasped and looked across at a frozen Finn. His wide eyes met mine. "At the risk of stating the obvious—I just hit something solid yet... soft."

I shuddered. He was still staring at me. I scrunched my face. "You want me to come over there and help, I suppose?" *Please say no. Please say no.*

"Yes, please. I didn't think it would be so hard, but... I'm rethinking our decision."

"Welcome to the club." I stood. "We're not doing this for us, though. Alfie will hopefully appreciate this when he finds out, and so will Donigal's wife and son. At least they'll know for sure."

"If this even is Donigal."

"We'll cross that crocodile-infested creek when we come to it." I went to his side before I lost my nerve. At least I had long sleeves to cover my nose and mouth. I knelt, and with one arm covering the lower half of my face, I trowelled away the dirt in the area his shovel had struck. After a minute, enough soil fell away to reveal dark plastic. I poked at it with my trowel. "Yep, soft and a bit squishy." I gagged. A rancid odour seeped around me. I quickly scrambled to my feet to get away from it.

"The shape looks head-like. I think you should do the reveal—you knew him better than me. As much as this is gross, I'm going to take a picture so we can confirm by looking at that rather than by crouching over the stinky body." I chucked my trowel on the ground. We'd forgotten to bring paper or plastic to wrap things in. I was not putting that trowel back in my bag.

He stared at the plastic I'd just revealed, horror on his face. "I don't want to do this. Maybe you're right—we should just call Bellamy now."

I gave him a look as I took my gloves off and put them on the ground. "We're doing this. All or nothing. Come on." I got the camera app up on my phone, ready for a pic, and I grabbed my torch, turned it on, and pointed it at the shape. "Let's just get it over and done with, and don't breathe in while you're down there, or you'll regret it."

His gaze moved to mine. Poor Finn. There was zero enthusiasm in his voice when he said, "Okay. Argh. Here I go." He sucked in a breath, held it, and knelt. He fumbled with the plastic long enough that he turned his head, took another breath, and kept going. After tugging and grunting—the plastic must've been thick—he ripped open a section. He stumbled back and fell on his bum. "Oh, Jesus. This is bad." He shuffled backwards on his bottom while I held my breath and stepped closer.

He wasn't wrong. As my torch shone on the ghastly, sallow face, I snapped a photo, then turned, narrowly avoiding Finn, and threw up.

We both moved away from the body, and I sent Carina a text saying we found the body. "Is it him? I think it looks like him, from what I can remember." I slid my phone into my back pocket and turned the torch off.

"Yes, I think it is too." Finn gagged but didn't vomit. "I'll call Bellamy."

Donigal's ghost appeared next to his grave, and I started. "They're coming. Get out of here, now!" What? "Hurry!" Oh, poop on stick. I listened intently for other people. A faint noise came from just over the rise, from towards the house.

"Finn, we have to get out of here now. Someone's coming."

"What?"

"Hurry, young lady. They'll kill you." Donigal jerked his head to look towards the house, then disappeared.

I grabbed Finn's hand. "There's no time. Call the police as we run." I pulled him along. There was no time to pick up the shovel and trowel, which was a shame because they would make good weapons, especially if whoever was coming was as intent on killing people as Donigal seemed to think.

I dropped Finn's hand when I knew he was onboard with my directive. We started to make our way back down the hill. We'd only gone about sixty feet when a gruff male voice came out of the darkness. "Not so fast. What are you doing here? Stop!"

My heart thudded hard, and adrenaline shot through me. I didn't recognise that voice, and I didn't think Finn did either because he moved faster, but we could only travel so fast on uneven ground with bad lighting.

Swearing drifted down, and it sounded like two men. Each time my gumboots slapped the ground, I waited for the hole that would turn my ankle again. Finn fumbled with his back pocket and breathed out, "I'm calling nine, nine, nine."

More swearing from behind and rustling. "Stop, trespassers!"

No. Freaking. Way. I wasn't stopping for anything.

"Police," Finn panted into the phone.

I risked glancing back. Two moving shapes weren't that far away. And they looked huge, at least Finn's height but beefier. Although, it might have been because I was scared, and they were higher up than us. Whatever it was, I didn't care. I just wanted to make it to the road. Ah all the wasps in hades— we'd reached the fence, but we weren't at the place we'd cut before. Finn was giving our position to whoever was on the phone. I chucked the torch into his backpack and pulled out the bolt cutters. My sweaty hands had difficulty finding purchase on the handles, and I fumbled trying to line the chopping part with the fence.

The men were closing in on us. Their galloping down the hill was louder.

*Snap.* One wire gone.

My breath rasped in and out of my throat while Finn explained our situation on the phone. Argh, trying to do precise stuff while freaking out wasn't easy.

*Snap.* Two wires gone.

We jumped over, but I didn't drop the cutters. We were going to need them again soon, and maybe I could hit one of the men with them if they caught up to us.

"Okay. Please hurry. We're being chased." He put his phone in his back pocket and kept jogging. He glanced behind. The men had reached the fence already. "They've gained on us."

When he looked ahead, I looked back. The two dark shapes were having trouble with the fence. They obviously hadn't seen where we'd cut it.

"Stop or I'll shoot!"

Finn and I both swore. I wanted so badly to dive on the ground, make myself smaller, but then they'd catch up to us.

Hitting a moving target in the dark wouldn't be easy for them, but there was always a lucky shot.

"Keep running," Finn panted out.

"Okay."

"Give me that." He grabbed the bolt cutters, and not carrying that awkward weight made a difference. I picked up the pace a bit.

"I'm going to get the torch out of your bag so we can run faster. They can see us enough by the moonlight, so I don't think it matters."

"Agreed." He slowed slightly while I dug into his bag.

"Got it." I clicked it on, and it made things easier. We both ran faster.

A crack exploded around us. My legs moved faster as panic pushed me on. They really were shooting at us. *Holy hades.* At least the noise hadn't been too similar to thunder or I might have lost the plot. As it was, my heart was beating way faster than it should be, even though I was running. Each footfall jarred my body. My backpack bounced manically against my back. Had one of us been shot? Would it hurt or would the adrenaline override the pain?

I couldn't know, and I wasn't stopping to find out. If I was still alive at the bottom of the hill, great.

We came to the next fence. Going down was way quicker than coming up.

Finn was more adept at cutting than I was. Another shot echoed, and we both ducked. I clicked the torch off. "Keep going. I'll watch them." I turned to see where they were. Now that they didn't have clear sight of us, they were scrambling over the other fence. We'd made a lot of distance on them at least.

"Done." Finn jumped up and went over but stopped to

make sure I'd cleared the fence before continuing. I turned the torch on again.

Sirens sounded in the distance. Please be our ride out of here.

My top stuck to me with sweat—I wasn't sure how much was from exertion and how much was from raging fear.

"We know who you are. Live in fear because we're coming for you." Another shot sounded. I risked a look back. They'd stopped. Had the sirens got them thinking it was time to make their own getaway? And who in hades were they?

I glanced back again. They turned and started back up the hill. I stopped running, sucking air into my screaming lungs. What if they got away? It wasn't anyone Finn or I recognised —so, not Danny Donigal, and the man helping his mum was too old to be running down hills in the dark. What if they did come for us later? But how did they know who we were? They couldn't have gotten a clear look at us in the dark. Maybe they could find out via the police, or maybe they were bluffing?

Stuff it. I wasn't letting them get away. I turned my torch off, sucked in another breath, and started back up the hill. I was lighter than them and hopefully fitter. If they tried to get away in a car, I at least wanted to get the number plate details. And what would they do about the body? Would they try and dig it up and take it with them? Surely they didn't have time. Unless there was another way off the farm than the main driveway.

I stayed low as I went—less chance of them seeing me if they glanced around. When I made it to the first fence, I found the hole we'd made and quickly climbed over. They were far enough ahead of me that they were navigating the next fence already. I stopped and crouched for a moment, because when they got over the fence, they might face my way for a moment.

When they'd cleared it with swearing and a couple of shouts of pain—ha ha, sucked in—I got going again, moving faster. If I hurt myself now, well, it didn't matter. They didn't know I was here, and I could hobble down the hill in my own time.

My phone vibrated in my back pocket with a message—I'd put it on silent before we came because I didn't think sneaking around with a noisy phone was the epitome of smart. It was Finn. *Where the hell are you? I get down near the road, and you're gone. Jesus, Avery!* There was nothing funny about the situation, but I grinned—he was so upset, he'd used my real name.

I sent back: *They could come after us later. Following them carefully to find out their number plate. Also seeing if they move the body.*

He sent back: *FFS!*

I slid my phone back in my pocket—the last thing I needed was for my phone light to give me away.

As I neared the next fence, I could just make out the men standing near the grave. They were probably discussing how long they had and whether they should move it or not. If I were them, I would run. Maybe there wasn't much, if any, evidence on the body, but how would they explain their presence here? The other thing that bothered me was how did they know Finn and I were here? Was it a coincidence? Maybe they'd chosen this exact time to come move the body?

I made it to the fence. Looked like they'd made up their minds. They hurried off the way they'd come—back towards the house. It took me a moment to find where I'd cut the fence last time; then I hopped over. Now that they were fleeing in earnest, I didn't think they'd turn around, so I clicked my torch on and ran to the grave area. I didn't stop when I got there. I followed the two thugs. Now they were over the slight rise, I'd lost sight of them.

Was Mrs Donigal in danger? What if she was home by herself?

I shone my torch ahead and moved faster. If I broke my leg, I wasn't going to be happy, but if I lost them, I'd be scared and even less happy. I didn't want psychopaths waiting for their opportunity to kill me. I only had one chance, so I had to risk it.

I made it to the top of the rise. There they were, outlined in the moonlight. I'd gained a bit more on them. Ignoring the fear skittering through my belly, I shone my torch ahead and closed the space between us. Hopefully they'd be breathing just as heavily as me and not hear me following.

My phone vibrated again. But I didn't have time to stop and read it, so I ignored it.

Then it vibrated constantly. Someone was trying to call. I slowed and pulled the phone out of my pocket. Bellamy's name was on the screen. I stopped, swiped to answer it, then started off again with it against my ear. "What is it?" I panted as quietly as I could.

"Winters, where are you?"

"At the top of the hill, chasing the two guys who shot at us. Where are you?" Was he already here, or was he calling from the station?

"I'm at the homestead with Finn and two more units. I want you to stop chasing them. We're heading towards you now."

"You'll take ages if you're on foot. It could be a fifteen-to-twenty-minute walk." An engine started. Oh, that's how they got here. "Ah, Sergeant, they've got wheels." Red tail lights shone over a hundred feet ahead of me. That's how they'd gotten to us so quickly. "It sounds like one of those quad-bike things." Argh! There was no way I could keep up with that. What if it was headed in a different direction than the house?

"Which way are they headed?"

"I think towards the house." I ran faster to keep them in view. The land sloped slightly down from where I was. Provided there were no other hills hiding in the distance, I could keep a visual on them. "Now they're veering a bit to the north."

"Okay. I have to hang up, but I'll call you back shortly. Keep them in your sights as long as you can."

"Will do."

He hung up, and I kept running. My legs were going to be sore tomorrow, but at least I'd be alive. It was too late for poor Mr Donigal. Hopefully this would all prove that Alfie had nothing to do with it. I couldn't see him being involved with people who owned guns, which were, incidentally, illegal over here as they were in Australia. It wasn't a shotgun they'd used. One of the men had raised one arm to shoot, and his body positioning indicated a handgun. I had no idea what different guns sounded like when fired, though, so I couldn't use that to decide what it was. Neither of the men looked like they were carrying anything as big as a shotgun.

Shame it was so dark though. There's no way I could pick out either of them in a line-up.

My phone buzzed again. I stopped, answered it, then kept running. "Hello, Sergeant. They're headed even more to the west."

"Okay, I have two cars headed around to close off the road that fronts the farm to the north. They might cross into one adjoining farm, which also only has access to that road. Stay there. I need you to show us where the body is. I have Donigal's son, Danny, firing up one of the farm vehicles now. The forensics team is on its way too."

"Okay. I have a torch with me. I'll hold it up so you can see where I am. I have a feeling the road access ends about a hundred feet west of where I am. Bye." I hung up and put my phone in my back pocket, then sighed. We were going to be safe. I stared up at the sky and shook my head. What a crazy night. Finn and I could've been killed, but we hadn't been, and we'd done what we set out to do. Poor Mrs Donigal and Danny. They'd start the grieving process now. All hope had dissolved like a snowflake in the rain, at least for them. I wondered what Alfie was going to say when Finn told him what he'd done for him.

The rumble of another engine and a pair of headlights came towards me. I held my flashlight above my head and angled it so it shone on the ground just in front of me. In another couple of minutes, the lights stopped moving, and the engine cut off. Three torches bobbing in the night turned into four men—Bellamy, Danny, and two police officers. Just as they reached me, I said, "This way."

I led them to the body, the stench of which had well and truly leaked into the atmosphere. I gagged, then looked at Danny. "Sorry."

His face looked pained, but he waved a dismissive hand. "It's okay."

"I'll just stand over here and wait a bit, let you get on with it."

After confirming for himself that yes, there was definitely a dead body, Bellamy looked at me. "Thank you, Avery." He looked at Danny. "Sorry to ask, lad, but is that your father?"

One of the officers shone his torch on the face, but I

turned away. I didn't need to see the details. "Yes, officer." Danny's heavy voice sounded gutted.

"Right," said Bellamy. "You shouldn't stay here. Can you take Avery back, please, Danny? When the forensics people arrive, I'll get you to show them here, if that's all right."

"It's fine by me, Sergeant." He turned, and I fell into step just behind him. It was as awkward as anything I'd ever done. We had nothing to talk about, didn't know each other, and what did you say to someone who'd just identified their dead father? I also didn't want to explain what I was doing traipsing around his property uninvited. Hopefully he wouldn't ask.

We reached the vehicle. It was an all-terrain thing with no doors and four seats. I turned my torch off and hopped into the front passenger seat. I would've preferred the back—to discourage any conversation—but it would've looked weird.

Danny got in and started the car. He did a u-ie and headed back towards the house. At least his driving was sedate and careful. "What were you doing on my farm?"

Satan's underpants. "Looking for your dad." Headlights came towards us—maybe the forensics team? He kept quiet until they passed us.

"Why would you do that? We don't even know you." He flicked a glance my way; then his expression changed to annoyance. "Oh, I get it. You're a journalist. You'll do anything to get a story."

The hairs on my arms rose, and anger niggled in my belly. "I was trying to help Alfie. Finn doesn't think he did it." I knew he knew Finn, so I didn't have to explain who was who.

"Of course he did it. My dad fired him. He smokes too many drugs. You know they make you schizto."

Okay, so he'd just seen his dad's body. Maybe it was bringing out the worst in him. "Um, drugs can cause mental illness, but a) Alfie doesn't have it, and b) just because someone has a mental illness doesn't mean they're violent."

"Well, he is."

He stopped the vehicle.

It was then my subconscious finally let me in on a little secret.

Ah, poop. I swallowed. I didn't have all the pieces of the puzzle, but a huge one just fell into place.

For confirmation, I clicked my torch on and shone it on his wrist. Argh! I then shone it into his eyes. "Why are we stopping?"

He put an arm up to protect his face. "You're getting out, journalist scum. You've caused enough trouble." He went to snatch the torch, but I was quicker and pulled it away. I had to wonder why he wanted me to get out here. That wasn't a good enough reason. And I thought I knew.

"Just take me as far as the house, please. Bellamy asked you to."

"I said, get out." His teeth were gritted together.

"What are you going to do if I get out?"

"Leave you here."

I had a feeling that if I got out, he'd run me over. It was the only weapon on hand, and it could be made to look like an accident.

He grabbed my hair with his left hand and yanked me towards him. Pain shot along my scalp. "If you won't get out, I'll do it." I swung the torch around wildly, trying to connect with his face or skull. Yes! "Argh!" He snatched the torch away and threw it. "Bitch!" I grabbed at his hands as he moved across and dragged me to his side of the car. Hades, that hurt. Testing my pain threshold, I let go with one hand and got my phone out of my pocket. I gripped it with my left hand. "Siri, call Bellamy on speaker."

"You sneaky trollop." He stopped pulling my hair and reached around my back to get the phone. I twisted my hand so far around my other side, that he'd have to release my hair so he could grab it with his other hand. The access wasn't good with the steering wheel in his way.

A muffled "hello" came from my phone.

I screamed, "Danny killed his father." As I yelled, "Help," Danny lifted his hand back and wound up, punching me in the cheek. This time my scream was raw pain. He was trying to grab my phone while I fought dizziness. *Don't give up. You survived lightning, Avery.* I threw my phone into the rear footwell of the car. Danny took the bait, probably thinking I was about to pass out—he wasn't wrong. It was all I could do to stay alert.

I smashed my hip on the handbrake while scrambling to a sitting positing in the driver's seat, but the pain was nothing compared to dying. It might even have woken me up a little bit.

Danny was leaning in the back of the car. Thank God the handbrake was where it was in a normal car. I released it and slammed on the accelerator.

Danny was half in, half out of the car. "Stop, you crazy trollop. Stop the car!" He cried out. I managed to strap my seat belt on as he climbed the rest of the way into the car. I hoped I'd hurt his legs so he couldn't do anything else to me, but I wasn't so lucky.

He put his hands around my throat. "Stop the car, or I'll choke you," he yelled over the wind and engine noise as he squeezed.

"You'll choke me anyway." I didn't want to crash the car,

but I wanted to get rid of him, so I jerked the wheel to the right, enough for his grip to come undone and fling him to the other side of the back seat. I was careful not to go too hard though because I could have flipped the whole thing on the rough gravel road. I corrected course towards the house. The lights were visible in the distance.

Stabbing pain shot from my cheek into my skull. Nausea rose up my throat. Bloody concussion. I needed ice and painkillers.

Danny grunted as he righted himself. This time, I slammed the brakes on. I had a seat belt; he didn't. He flew forward, his chest hitting the back of the front seat. Shame there was no headrest, or I would've gotten a two-for-one deal and we'd have equal concussions. I floored it and took off again.

He grabbed my hair again. I slammed on the brakes, then accelerated, then broke, then accelerated. His head was whiplashing all over the place. I started laughing. Maybe I was as crazy as he thought.

Blue-and-red lights came towards us. I accelerated one last time and undid my seat belt. Then I slowly stopped the car, pulled the keys out of the ignition, and flew out. There was nothing else Danny could do, unless he wanted to strangle me in front of the police.

He fell out and ran. The police car reached me and came to a halt. They jumped out and chased him down. After the taxi-driver stop-start treatment I'd given him, he wasn't too steady on his feet. They tackled him and slapped cuffs on him. Thank goodness Bellamy believed my phone call, although Danny made himself look more suspicious by running. He was his own worst enemy.

The police had him in custody, so it was safe for me to

retrieve my phone, which I did. It was still on the call, and I lifted it to my ear. "Hello?"

"Ms Winters?" It was Bellamy.

"Yes. Your guys got here and arrested Danny."

"Stay where you are. I'll be there in a moment."

"Yes, Sergeant."

One of the police who arrested Danny, put him in the police car while the other one came over to me. "Are you all right?" He stared at my cheek. "That could be broken." The police headlights were still on and obviously lighting my shiner up like a Christmas tree.

"Oh, yeah." I'd forgotten about it. I mean, it was throbbing, as was my head, but there was other stuff to concentrate on.

"There's an ambulance attending. We can give you a ride back to the house."

"Sergeant Bellamy is coming. I'll wait for him, then get myself over there."

His brow wrinkled. "I'll wait with you."

"Thanks."

Bellamy arrived within two minutes. Before talking to me, he went to the police car and had a chat to the officers and Danny. I had time to think through the pounding pain while I waited for Bellamy. I had a gazillion questions. He finally made his way back to me. His eyes widened when he got a decent look at my cheek. "Jeeze, Winters, that's gotta hurt. What happened?"

"Danny punched me. He was trying to get my phone, and I wouldn't let him. I managed to call you. He didn't like that. I think he killed his father."

His brows drew together. "Why? Other than his behaviour

just now—which I'll take a statement about later tonight—
what makes you think that?"

"I saw Donigal arguing in the street on the morning before
he went missing."

"With his son?"

"No, with his neighbour—Barnaby Killeen, or, as you
know him, Graham Field."

His eyes narrowed. "Is he the one you wouldn't tell me
about?"

"Yes. He's done jail time for attempted murder of a
previous neighbour. When he got out, he changed his name."

"So where does Danny fit in, and how did you come to be
trespassing on this farm looking for a body? Finn filled me in
on a couple of things."

Thank goodness because I needed to get this information
out and sit down. Come to think of it. "Mind if I sit?"

He started. "Oh, sorry. Please do."

I plonked my bottom into the driver's seat of Danny's car
thing. "Anyway, while Donigal was arguing with Killeen, he
was waving his arms around, and he gave him the finger. This
brought attention to the bling on his wrist. I noticed his gold
watch and thought it odd that a man dressed like a farmer—in
worn work clothes—would bother wearing such an expensive-
looking watch. But you guys found a watch at Alfie's. I
assumed it was that one. When we came to your office, I was
preoccupied. I saw a picture of a watch on your corkboard."

"The one we found at Alfie's was silver in colour. It's actually stainless steel, and we got confirmation from Danny that it
was the watch his dad had been wearing the night he went
missing. Are you saying he's lying?"

"Yes. I saw the watch on Danny tonight, and I realised
he'd been wearing it just after his dad went missing as well—I

ran into him at the café. It all clicked when he slowed the car down and wanted me to get out here." And when I remembered that Mr Donigal had emotionally said he couldn't believe "he" could kill him. *He* was obviously his son, and not the two goons who shot at Finn and me, and not Alfie. Besides, I couldn't see Alfie digging a hole and burying Donigal, then making it back to his place for a thorough clean and a good sleep in that time. There was no way.

"He what? Why? Did you accuse him?"

"Not at that stage. He was upset at me being a journalist. I thought it was weird just how upset he was. Then when I saw the watch, it clicked. Look, I could've been wrong, but his reaction when I wouldn't get out sealed the deal. He grabbed my hair and tried to drag me out of the car." A particularly excruciating throb lanced through my cheek, and I winced, which made it hurt more. "I want to know who those two guys were who shot at us though. I'm not sure how it all fits together."

"You and me both, Winters, but right now, let's get you to hospital. That might be broken. Come to think of it, I'll come to the hospital later to get your statement, and I'll fill you in as soon as I know what's what. I owe you that much."

I gave him a wan smile. "Thanks, Sergeant." My phone buzzed with a call. "It's Vinegar. I'd better take it." For the first time ever, I witnessed Bellamy smirk. Hmm, interesting. "Hey, Vinegar."

"Where the hell are you? They just drove past with Danny in the back of the car. Did he faint at the sight of his dad or something?"

"No. He tried to kill me, or at least thoroughly hurt me. My cheek's a bit sore, so I'm coming back with Bellamy now and going to hospital."

"Seriously. I couldn't believe it when I got near the bottom, and YOU WEREN'T THERE!" I moved the phone away from my ear. Bellamy gave me a sympathetic look.

"No need to get all shouty. I couldn't let them get away, or we'd be in trouble later. Anyway, I'll see you in a minute. Bye." I didn't wait for his goodbye. "Here, Sergeant." I handed him the keys to the farm vehicle.

"This can stay here. We'll have to include this in the investigation now. Assault, attempted murder. Even if he didn't kill his father, he's going to be facing some hefty charges. Hop in my car. I've borrowed it from forensics." I followed him to the dark sedan, and he opened the door for me.

I slipped into the seat and shut my eyes. A chill caressed my cheek, and a male voice came from the back of the car, but I didn't turn, for obvious reasons.

"Thank you for everything, young lady. What's happened has broken my heart, but at least my wife will be safe now." A white glow momentarily enveloped me, and the coldness disappeared. Seemed as if being stingy and not paying your debts wasn't enough to keep you out of heaven. At least his wife could live more comfortably now, except it was too little too late. She had to live with the knowledge that her son killed her husband. How depressing.

Bellamy started the car and drove carefully. It was a much calmer ride than when I was driving. The sergeant's phone rang. He answered it… while driving. Naughty, naughty. He put it in the holder on the dash on speaker. "Bellamy speaking."

"Sergeant, it's PC Feather. Mr Donigal is complaining that Ms Winters assaulted him with the car. Apparently she was driving in a manner as to cause him to almost fall out and strike his chest, also he's complaining of whiplash. Do you want to arrest her too?"

Despite the pain in the general vicinity of my head, I started laughing.

Bellamy glanced at me. "Winters, please explain." So I did. By the time I finished, Bellamy and PC Feather were both in hysterics, and we'd reached the house. Bellamy got off the phone and helped me to the ambulance, where Finn waited, his arms crossed. He scowled at me as I approached, but once I reached the back of the open ambulance and the light hit my face, his mouth fell open. His arms dropped to his sides, and he ran over.

"Jesus, Lightning. What the hell happened?"

I shrugged. "I'll fill you in on the way to the hospital. Wanna come?"

I couldn't decipher the look in his eyes, but it was intense, and my stomach flipped. Gah, not now, hormones. "Of course I'll come." His voice was a lot quieter than normal. "I want to make sure you're okay."

"Lightning couldn't kill me, Vinegar. Danny didn't stand a chance." I grinned. Big mistake. *Ow*!

# CHAPTER 11

Two days after our night at the farm, Finn, Carina, and I sat at Bellamy's desk, the apple tart I'd made sitting on it. We'd asked if Carina could attend because she'd been part of our investigation, too, and we didn't want to tell her everything all over again. They'd kept me overnight in hospital because of my concussion, but X-rays showed my cheek wasn't broken. Nevertheless, the next morning when I came out, she insisted on coming to get me, and she stayed and worked from my place all day to make sure I was fine. To be honest, I was kind of glad she did because I slept the whole day, and if I did die, no one would've known for ages. Mrs Crabby would've had a conniption if my body stunk up her apartment.

Bellamy rested his arms on the table, his demeanour professional but somewhat relaxed. Fingers crossed he had the whole story to tell us. "I can't believe I'm going to say this but thank you, Avery and Finn, for sticking your noses in where they didn't belong. Thanks to you both, an innocent man will be going free, and the real culprits have been arrested."

"Yay!" Carina clapped. "I'm so proud of you bot'."

I smiled. "Thanks. And thanks for helping us."

She rolled her eyes. "I didn't do anyt'ing, except sit at Finn's and worry my behind off."

Bellamy looked at her. "No, it was good that someone knew what they were up to. The way things went, they easily could've been killed or kidnapped, and we wouldn't have known anything about it or where it happened." He gave me, then Finn dirty looks.

Fox appeared behind Bellamy. "Good work, Avery. He's right, though. You took a huge risk. I wish you would be more careful." I gave him a subtle smile and a look that suggested it might very well happen again. He frowned and shook his head.

"I appreciate the lecture, I really do, but please tell us what you found out." Everyone stared at me, Finn and Carina chuckling.

Eventually, Bellamy broke and grinned. "You're always going to be impossible, aren't you?"

"I can't promise anything, but yes." I grinned.

"Right, well, after we arrested the two men who shot at you and identified them, we recognised them from a drug bust we did three years ago. They're guys who've been in and out of jail their whole lives. I happen to know that Alfie partakes of marijuana occasionally, and I happen to know these guys supply the local market. I admit to being a bit sneaky because he hadn't said anything about those guys in the first place, I wondered if he'd been scared. I told him they shot you, Finn, and that you might die."

Finn's mouth fell open. "Oh my God, you didn't."

"It's a good thing I did, because the whole story came out about how he'd introduced them to Donigal about growing something on the farm. They never actually told him it was drugs, and even though he thought it might be, he didn't ask. Donigal refused, of course. His son, on the other hand, promised to make it happen. He was sick of his dad with-holding money. That night, Danny got into an argument with his father about it after his dad got home from the pub. They got into an altercation, and Danny's story is that he was defending himself and punched his father, accidentally killing him. He called those guys in a panic and asked them to help get rid of the body, and if they did, he'd guarantee the crops could be grown on their farm—they were looking at setting up a massive hydroponics shed. They knew you were there because there was a noise-activated camera in the wood pile. They wanted to make sure the grave wasn't disturbed." Well, that answered the question about whether them finding us was luck or not.

"I have to ask a question."

Bellamy looked at me. "Yes."

"We found out that there's no loan on the farm, and when I interviewed Mrs Donigal, I'll be honest, they looked poor, but we're thinking maybe they aren't as poor as Mr Donigal liked to make out. What's the story there?"

He stared at me for a beat too long, probably tossing up whether to tell us or not. "Well, this is confidential information, but you've done so much for this case that if you promise not to repeat this in any way, shape, or form, I'll tell you."

"I promise." That was a no-brainer.

"I promise too," said Finn.

Carina nodded. "So do I."

"Mr Donigal had over eight hundred thousand pounds

squirrelled away in two different bank accounts, neither of which his wife or son had access to. He was frugal to the extreme, and often his wife had to make do with a small amount of money for groceries and the like. Quite sad, actually. When I told her, I think it broke her heart, well, broke it more, considering her son killed her husband. She didn't react well."

Finn shook his head. "That's awful. And that shop needs to be paid too, and Mr Field, or whatever his name is. How many other debts are outstanding?"

"We've recorded about forty-two thousand."

"Yikes." I couldn't imagine owing that much money for incidental stuff. I doubt I'd ever be in possession of that amount of money or assets, let alone have over eight hundred thousand pounds to play with. Sheesh.

Bellamy took a sip of water. "So, all three are in gaol, and we have a good case against them. You two will have to be witnesses at trial. I hope you don't have a problem with that."

I shook my head. "Nope."

"Of course not." Finn's tone left no doubt.

"There's one more thing." Bellamy stood, went to the door, and opened it. He said, "Come in," to someone standing outside.

Alfie came through the door, and as soon as he saw Finn, he grinned and teared up. Finn jumped up. "Alfie!" The men hugged.

"Finn, dude, you saved my life. I'm so sorry I wasn't upfront with the police from the get-go. Those dealers are bad news, and I knew I'd be toast if I said anything."

"It's okay, man. I understand completely. You did what you had to."

"Well, thank you. You've saved me twice now. One day, I'll figure out how to make it up to you."

"Just stay safe."

He nodded. "I will." Alfie looked past Finn to me. "I understand I have you to thank as well."

I smiled, my cheek aching for a moment. "Yes, but I was happy to. Finn and Carina were convinced you were innocent, and I trust them, so I figured it would be remiss of me to let this go."

"Well, I owe you a debt of gratitude too. One of these days, I'll pay you back."

"Alfie, just live your best life. That'll make Finn and me super happy."

"You'll be happy to know I've taken the first step. As of today, I'm off all the drugs and alcohol. One of my mates has a job for me at a nursery too. I start next week."

"Brilliant, young man." Bellamy's expression was one of respect. Maybe he thought as I did—Alfie had had a few setbacks in his life, yet he wasn't going to give up.

"Ooh, I know." Carina sat up straight, enthusiasm in her tone. "Why don't we take a photo of you t'ree for the paper? You're still writing an article, aren't you, Avery?"

"Yes, I am."

"Give me your phone." I got my phone out of my bag, unlocked it, and handed it to her. "Oh, you have a different phone to me. How do I work this?" She mucked around with it for a moment, then sucked in a breath. She touched the screen with two fingers, enlarging the image on it. "Oh, my lord!" She put one hand on her mouth and started laughing. She stared at me incredulous. "Did you paint d'is, Avery?"

"Huh, paint what?" She faced the phone screen towards me, and Finn looked at it over my shoulder. Oh. My. Word.

Finn sucked in a breath, and his voice was loud. "What the heck, Avery? That's me?! That's not me. What the heck is this? What is it doing on your phone?" I looked at him, and he looked at me as if I was some kind of sicko.

I burst out laughing. "Oh my God, I'm so sorry. Ms Pearce, an artist, did it. I interviewed her about her art a few days ago, and she had pictures of you, Bailey, and a few other men on her wall that I'm sure didn't pose for her. She takes secret photos of people's faces, then puts them on naked bodies. I was going to tell you and Bailey, but I didn't know how."

Alfie snorted. "And I thought I had problems." That earned more laughter from Carina and me.

Finn looked concerned. "I feel violated."

Bellamy peered at the picture. "At least she's been generous, son. It could've been worse."

Finn stared at Bellamy. "Can you charge her with something, make her burn that painting?"

"I'm afraid not. She's not breaking any laws."

"Creepy old lady." Finn deleted the picture, then handed my phone back. "At least you can't drool over it now."

I put one hand on my good cheek. "Oh, poo, however will I enjoy my alone time?"

Finn's eyes had mischief in them when he looked at me. "The real thing's so much better."

Carina rolled her eyes. "Worst pick-up line ever, Finn. You won't catch mermaids with fish bait."

Bellamy, who'd been watching the exchange with abject horror in his eyes, clapped once. "Okay, debriefing's over. I never want to hear about that painting again. Go on and enjoy your lives." He looked at Alfie. "Especially you, young man.

From now on, keep in touch, and if anyone gives you trouble, I'll handle it."

The appreciation on his face was there for all to see. "Thank you, Sergeant."

"Hey, we haven't taken the photo yet." Carina held her hand out for my phone. I set it up for her properly this time and gave it back.

"All you have to do is press that red button."

She giggled. "Okay, I t'ink I can do d'at." Alfie stood in between Finn and me, and we put our arms around each other's backs. "Say buttocks!"

⚜

If you enjoyed *A Fallow Grave*, you might want to grab book 4, *A Frozen Stiff*, which is out 23rd June, 2022.

And if you're looking for more cosy mysteries and haven't tried my Paranormal Investigation Bureau series yet, why not grab *Witchnapped in Westerham*.

**All it takes is one morning for Sydney Photographer Lily Bianchi's life to go off the rails and over a cliff.**

A well-dressed English woman turns up at her door, swearing she's a witch. If that's not crazy enough, she explains Lily's brother, James, has been kidnapped and the Paranormal Investigation Bureau needs Lily's help finding him. And the craziest part? The Englishwoman tells Lily she's a witch too.

Before she can say, "Where's my coffee?" she's on a plane bound for Westerham, England. Unfortunately, England's not as welcoming as she hoped--she's barely arrived before she gets set up, arrested, and almost shot.

Things can only get better from here, right? Yeah, right...

# ALSO BY DIONNE LISTER

(Paranormal Cosy Mystery)

*A Killer Welcome #1*

*A Regrettable Roast #2*

*A Fallow Grave #3*

*A Frozen Stiff #4 Coming 23rd June 2022*

## **The Circle of Talia**

(YA Epic Fantasy)

*Shadows of the Realm*

*A Time of Darkness*

*Realm of Blood and Fire*

## **The Rose of Nerine**

(Epic Fantasy)

*Tempering the Rose*

# ABOUT THE AUTHOR

USA Today bestselling author, Dionne Lister is a Sydneysider with a degree in creative writing, two Siamese cats, and is a member of the Science Fiction and Fantasy Writers of America. Daydreaming has always been her passion, so writing was a natural progression from staring out the window in primary school, and being an author was a dream she held since childhood.

Unfortunately, writing was only a hobby while Dionne worked as a property valuer in Sydney, until her mid-thirties when she returned to study and completed her creative writing degree. Since then, she has indulged her passion for writing while raising two children with her husband. Her books have attracted praise from Apple iBooks and have reached #1 on Amazon and iBooks charts worldwide, frequently occupying top 100 lists in fantasy and mystery.

Printed in Great Britain
by Amazon

24302821R00121